In the Aura of Tulips
在郁金香的光泽中

徐怀静 ◎ 著

华夏出版社
HUAXIA PUBLISHING HOUSE

目录
contents

— 上篇 —

致周炯槃教授　For Professor Zhou Jiongpan / 002

致林中教授　For Professor Lin Zhong / 006

毕业季的礼物　The Gift upon Graduation / 014

毕业季的念珠　Beads of the Graduation Season / 018

毕业季的歌　Song of the Graduation Season / 022

白塔　Pagoda / 028

尼泊尔　Nepal / 030

拉萨的天空下　Under the Sky of Lhasa / 034

在布达拉宫的翅膀下　Beneath the Wings of Podala / 036

外星人　Jack from another Star / 038

念珠　Beads / 040

我要带着一把剪刀来见你　I'm Coming to You with a Pair of Scissors / 042

你的快乐　Your Happiness / 046

我为你写诗　I Write Poems for You / 050

最后一次见到你　The Last Time I Saw You / 052

在郁金香的光泽中　In the Aura of Tulips / 054

致信仰　For Faith / 056

告诉你或不告诉你　To Tell You or Not / 058

写在母亲节　On Mother's Day / 060

五月的多伦多　Toronto in May / 062

在那拉提的草原上　On Nalati's Grassland / 068

半地下室的春天　My Spring / 072

在城市的掩护下　Under the Cover of a City / 076

藏地的小女孩　The Little Tibetan Girl / 078

送别　Seeing You off / 082

静坐　Meditating / 084

失去父亲的女儿　A Fatherless Daughter / 086

我的燃灯节　My Butter Lamp Day / 090

我是冲动的风　I am the Wind, so Impulsive / 094

我是一名来自内地的小孩　I am an Inland Child / 096

饮茶时光　Tea Time / 098

让我　Let Me / 104

给胡建　Dearest / 106

写在情人节　On Valentine's Day / 108

在瓦尔登湖为你挑选的明信片　Choosing a Postcard for you in Concord / 110

枫树　Maple Trees / 114

当郊外的栀子花盛开　When Gardenia Flowers Bloomed in the Suburb / 116

夜驾　Night Driving / 120

又是秋天　Autumn Again / 122

梦　Dream / 124

我建造了一艘看不见的飞船　I Built an Invisible Spaceship / 126

在海的那一边　On the other Side of the Ocean / 128

我曾经拥有一个诵读者　I once Had a Reader / 130

左岸酒店　FX Hotel / 134

我在地铁里如是想　Thus do I Think in the Subway / 138

馈赠　Endowment / 140

第一次听见你说话　The First Time I Heard You Speak / 142

圣殿饮茶　Drinking Tea at a Holy Monastery / 144

我对你生起的心　The Heart for You that I Rise to / 146

蓝天 白雪 红袍　Azure Sky, White Snow, Red Kasaya / 148

—— 下篇 ——

致六祖 / 152

踩着厚厚的积雪，我来五台山看您 / 154

白塔山下 / 156

日记，暴雨 / 158

重回布达拉 / 160

我不认识你 / 162

想起你 / 164

我跨越了无量的海拔和你相遇 / 165

曾经 / 166

灵光古刹 / 168

五台山 / 170

各莫之旅 / 172

在雪域 / 175

给小阿克 / 177

定格 / 179

你零点来信 / 180

猫的独白 / 182

那时的我 / 184

秋日雨夜 / 185

致俗女 / 186

奔向拉卜楞 / 188

断灭 / 189

接受 / 190

妮妮的独白 / 191

栀子花 / 193

地形图 / 196

20 岁的礼物 / 198

情人 / 200

暴雨没有降临 / 202

归宿 / 204

我在时光广场等你 / 205

照片 / 207

给青江 / 209

最后一课 / 212

西蜀江边盼日出 / 214

想起苏东坡,在春风并不沉醉 / 216

的夜晚 / 217

道歉 / 219

给 Justine / 220

给婆(1) / 222

给婆(2) / 224

给贾斯汀——关于《英国病人》 / 226

序 曲

怀着一颗宁静感恩的心,我谱写这篇小小的序曲。

这本诗集跨越了我的四个"光年",让我在谱写"序曲"的一瞬间,顿悟:每一首诗,几乎都是情绪风暴的产物;好的诗都充满了悖论;太阳底下,没有什么新鲜事。诗人的工作不是去寻找新鲜的情感,而是将日常的情感,以不一样的方式表达为一首诗;诗歌要逃避个性,但只有在存在个性与情感的前提下,才谈得上"逃避";诗都是带着"影响的焦虑"之下的独白。

希望我的诗,有着浪漫主义诗歌的单纯和直接。希望我的诗,能具备现代主义诗歌在表达上的间接性和转换性。

希望我,能带着个性和传统不断地行走。 希望我,能变得无我。只沉浸在自我里的诗人,注定是一个没有生命力的诗人。常常思考这个问题:当年上海滩那个时尚的、离经叛道的少女如何蜕变成了一个朴素、简单、无我的学者、诗人、教师?

这本诗集，实现了我的良师益友 Gary Harmon 对我的希望。他在世时，不止一次地说过希望有一天我能出一本诗集。

感谢北京师范大学章燕教授，她的博学、低调、高贵的人品，是我今生的榜样。感谢她的诗歌课堂、文论课堂；感谢她每一次为我的小诗打分，鼓励着我一首首写下去。我的上述文字，部分直接来自我在章老师课堂上的笔记。

感谢我的同事卢志鸿。她传奇的身世、高贵的人品、横溢的才华，是我北邮生活中的一抹亮光和慰藉。

感谢陆建德老师，2005-2006 年他看了我写的很多英语诗后，就吩咐我要把这些诗收集起来。也许，陆老师在那时候就已经识别出我在这方面小小的"天分"？遗憾的是，本书只收集了我最近 4 年的创作。

本诗集里的所有诗，都来自"格来格来"公众号。感谢我的学生周桐和 Sunny。18 岁的 Sunny 陪伴着我创作了很多首诗。周桐为我申请了"格来格来"（藏文慢慢来之意）原创诗歌公众号，也是我诗歌创作的第一个读者和支持者。这本诗集，承载着我们很多的记忆。感谢我的西藏小女孩措姆，感谢我的西藏"小白马"白马扎西。格来格来公众号（gelaigelaij）配备了该诗集中所有作品的原创文字、摄影图片和我的原声朗读。

感谢拉卜楞的老师。感谢 Jack，感谢呷衣寺的扎西老师。

感谢我的编辑韩平，她是我第一本专著的编辑，也是我第一本诗集的编辑。

感谢北京邮电大学。

感谢这个世界，我爱你。

2018 年 7 月 30 日

上篇

致周炯槃教授

直到您已成为一尊铜像
被安放在青青草坪上
我才来寻找您
在夜晚的校园里

黑暗中我迷失
在往昔的坟地里
我穿行
一圈又一圈
仍然找不到您
直到有莘莘学子
将我牵引

记得
您离开的那一个清晨
我带着学生们来到您的像前告别
那时我还未完全明白
您对我的意义

直到我后来
走遍黄河长江、雪域高原、丝绸之路
只为寻觅那灯塔
照亮和驱散我今生的迷雾和黑暗

For Professor Zhou Jiongpan

I didn't find you in the darkness
Until you finally become a bronze bust
Silently Sitting on the lawn

But I had been lost
On the campus, a former graveyard
Circumambulating again and again
I couldn't find you
Until one student showed me
The path to your statue

That morning
When you passed away
In the memorial hall on the campus
I was the first one to lead the students to say farewell to you
But I didn't realize
What you meant to me then

Till later
I have traveled across the Yellow and Yangtze river,
Around the land of snow and along the silk road
To seek the lighthouse which could illuminate the darkness
And dispel the mists in my life

直到我
明白了馈赠的含义
我才顿悟
您为北邮学子留下的终身积蓄
才是我身边最纯洁崇高的布施

在浓浓的夜色中
我走过白色之楼
来找寻您

因为您的守护
今生我也将无畏无惧地
在这白色之楼下
度过我人生最好的时光

直到您走后
我才来寻找您

在夜色中
将手和前额放在您的铜像前
向您膜拜顶礼
一切不算太迟
我终于找到了您

2016.9

When I finally understood
The meaning of charitable act
I realized the purity and sublimity of your bestowment:
The dedication of your whole life's saving to
The buds of the future
The noblest charitable act I ever knew

In the thick darkness
I passed the white building
To look for you

Because of your guarding
I will dedicate my best time to BUPT
Under that white building

Only after you left
Did I come to look for you

In the night's darkness
I put my hands on your bust
And lowered my forehead
To pay my homage
It was not too late
Because I finally found you

致林中教授

我是一只富态的流浪猫
我的毛长得恣意霸气
布莱德是我的家
它的英文名字是刀刃 Blade
取这个名字的是我的主人

我生活的地方雾霾深重
但我的主人林中教授
能使天空湛蓝
空气清新

主人从不摇曳任何宗教的旌旗
他拒绝任何宗教的任何条款
主人的慈悲伟大胜过很多贴着标签的人
主人善行无数 布施无量

主人完成过无数巨大的工程项目
布莱德客户无穷 订单无数
主人为无根的学生们巨额捐助
主人过着全校最简朴的生活
他用的是非智能的黑白小手机
他没有汽车 更无豪宅
住的仍然是学校的宿舍

For Professor Lin Zhong

Though homeless, I am a plump cat
My hair grows freely and wildly
Blade is my home
And the name given by my master

The place where I live is always plunged in smog
But my master Professor Li Zhong
Can make the sky blue and air fresh

My master never flings any flag of religion
And he rejects any badges and names
But his compassion and charity have surpassed those of any titular man

My master has completed many grand projects
Blade has numerous clients and orders
My master has donated unlimited amount to the poor students
But he himself lives a very simple life
Still using the first generation cell phone
With no car and no big house

在结缘我的主人之前
来自高海拔的学生们
在这个校园里醉氧
常以二锅头和殴打来宣泄孤独

我的主人将他们带到布莱德
布施给他们爱
布莱德成了他们的家园
他们献给主人的哈达比献给活佛的还多

真的
我的主人能做到的
活佛不一定能做到

这个校园有好多大老板
可是
我们这些流浪猫都知道
活菩萨只有一个
那就是我的主人

有一天
来了一个雪云静珠
她善良虔诚
希望我的主人能像高僧大德一样
为她拨开迷雾
指明人生的意义和真谛

Before I knew my master
Those students from the plateau
Exhilarated in the sufficiency of the lowland's oxygen
Tended to get into trouble while drunk in an attempt
To release their loneliness

My master took them to Blade
Supported them to hold various meaningful activities
Since then Blade has become their homeland
They dedicated far more Tibetan Hada to my master than to their Lama

Surely
What my master did
Is beyond what a Rinpoche can do

There are many big bosses on this campus
But we homeless cats all know
My master is the only living Bodhisattva

One day came a lady named Pearl,
She was pure and tranquil as the highland's cloud and snow
Kind and Pious as she was,
She hoped my master to show her the real meaning of life in smog

主人感动于静珠的虔诚
和她以及她的丈夫共进午餐
但我的主人绝不装玄弄虚

谈到死亡
主人说希望在做项目的时候死去

主人说
他有位学生叫扎西
在主人的鼓励下读完了硕士学位
主人当时对扎西说：
"如果能继续攻读博士学位
扎西你不必有任何经济顾虑。"

主人对静珠说：
"如果你去西藏，
我让扎西当你的本地导游。"

主人还说
在半个世纪以前那场龙卷风中
他就已经决定：
专注工程
脱离行政

Moved by Pearl's Piety
Master dined with her and her husband
But master never pretended to be mysteriously profound

When it comes to death
He hopes he would pass away in the process of a project mission

Master said
He had a Tibetan student named Tash
Master hoped him
To continue his doctoral program upon his master's
Without worrying about financial back up

Master told Pearl
If she pays a visit to Tibet
Tash would be glad to be her local guide

Master also said
As early as half a century ago when there was a tornado
He had determined to concentrate on projects
And shun administration work

我是一只能读懂人心的猫
那一天
我看见雪云静珠凝视着我主人
她拜见过很多活佛
但她最佩服的是我的主人

我原来瘦骨嶙峋 颠沛流离
经常遭人殴打
后来命运之神开始善待我
自从那一天
从那小小的门缝
我溜进林中教授的布莱德

2018.4

As a cat I can read human mind
That day
I saw Pearl gazing at my master
She had visited many lamas
But the one she really admired was my master

I used to be skinny and emaciated
As a vagrant cat, I was always beaten by people
But the day when I slipped into Professor Lin Zhong's Blade
From the door's crack
Fate has started to favor me

毕业季的礼物

习惯了,象牙塔里无知无畏者的暴戾和矢石
习惯了,沙龙沦为露天舞会
习惯了,程序化的留言、书写、拍摄
习惯了,别离的难舍、随后的淡忘

惊讶于,这一朵花勇敢、娇艳、清丽
远方的建筑师眺望到她
即刻放下一切来找寻
这个时代最美、最博学、最勇敢的少女

习惯了,看他们进入象牙塔,拾级而上,成为过客
习惯了,看他们的大脑程序化
习惯了,他们的多情和无情

惊讶于
她说她要和我一样真诚
她说我是她在象牙塔里的最爱
她说她和我长得很像

习惯了,不再对美说,我爱你
惊讶于这最美的花
因我而升起无限信心

The Gift upon Graduation

Tired of being put at the mercy of the scrupulous idiots in the ivory tower
Tired of the Salon reduced to an open air ball
Tired of the silence and fury in the season of graduation
The programmed farewell message, posing and shooting
The lingering the oblivion
And the flashback when the present fades into the past

Surprised at such a delicate and charming flower
So fearless and ethereal
The most beautiful maiden of her time
Architects afar caught a glimpse of her
And came to her for inspiration

Tired of watching them entering the broken tower
Climbing the flights of stairs programed and brain-washed
Then departing
Tired of their coquettishness and ruthlessness
And the dimness in cave

Amazed at this undaunted maiden
So transparent and opaque
At the convocation ceremony
She submitted a painting of deep blue
On the canvas stars were flying across the night's sky
Stood a woman in revolutionary solitude

To beauty, I always refrain from saying I love you
Surprised at this beautiful flower
Shedding tears for me
And from me arising her faith

别离的那一天
她留下的不是程序
而是一副熠熠发光的蓝色油画
墨蓝的夜空中飞着无数的星星
夜色中伫立着一个女人
浸染着革命和孤独

多年以后才明白
那个深蓝色夜空下的女人
是我的画像
少女在毕业季的馈赠

2016.5

She said she would be as open and honest as I am
She said I was her most beloved one in the ivory tower
She said we resembled each other

On the last day of June
She gave me a farewell gift
A painting of deep blue

Many years later
I suddenly understood
That lonely and resilient woman
Under the blue sky of deep night
Is the portrait of myself
It consumed the girl 4 years
——her ultimate bestowment
On the last day of the graduation season

毕业季的念珠

让我在毕业季
送给你一串圣洁的念珠
来自于经书的深海

我诵读过无数诗歌
用各种语言
在四季的斜阳里,微风中

那一日
杂草丛生的花园
闭目冥想的我
用梵音将《心经》念诵

一首首的经文
一遍遍的咒语
就像一颗颗洁白的念珠
被晨曦中金色的光串起
美丽的公主被召唤和感动

她递给我历史的望远镜
我们漫步在 500 年前的星空
她说清代皇家的女子都很美丽
但只有最坚强智慧的格格
才能得到皇上的册封

Beads of the Graduation Season

In the month of graduation
Let me give you a string of white beads
Coming from the deep sea of holy scriptures

I have chanted many poems
In different languages
In the slanted sunlight, in the breeze

That day
In the unweeded garden
In mediation I chanted the Heart Sutra in Sanskrit

Sutra after sutra
Mantra after mantra
Like white beads
Threaded by a string of golden light
The beautiful princess was summoned and touched

She handed me the telescope of history
We sauntered through the Qing Dynasty
She said the princesses then were all handsome
But only those with strength and wisdom
Were eligible for the imperial title

厌倦了这个时代太自由
惊讶于清代的格格
深宫里每天必抄经书
皇上随意将她馈赠给功臣的儿子
一个从未谋面的男人
婚姻只是爱情的开始

她不是历史的沉香屑
她娇嫩、高贵、坚强不屈
有着游牧民族的离散视域
浸淫着历史的宿命、淡定
她有着最高贵敏感的心最真切的情
但绝不轻易流露

康熙帝的八世孙女
在六月的微风中
在故宫的城墙下
我送给你一串
被音乐和金线串起的圣洁佛珠

2016.5

Tired of the freedom of this age
And surprised by the Princesses in the Qing Dynasty
Who had to copy the sutra by hand in the palace everyday
And would be bestowed to the son of an accomplished official
Marriage marked the beginning of love

Is she the remaining incense of history ?
So delicate, noble and adamant
With the diasporic view of the nomads,
Fatalistic and detached
She has the most noble and sensitive heart,
The most authentic affection,
which she always held private herself

The 8th generation grandchild of Emperor Kangxi
In the breeze of the 6th month
Outside the imperial palace
I gave you a string of holy beads
Threaded by music and sunlight

毕业季的歌

毕业季芳草萋萋的校园
我们漫步在槐树间
姑娘说:"老师您真美,
让我为您拍下照片。"

空气中有着某种物质
让她的镜头无法将我定格
汨罗江上的迷惘就像校园的雾霾

思忖了很久
屈原为何跳入汨罗江
我明白历史只是少女的脸颊
这位爱国诗人是否知道
2000年以后
国家会"疆界模糊"
人们会"身份杂糅"

我们走过那幢白色的楼
谈起中外诗歌中
个人如何穿行于历史的飘带

谈到眼下的分离
姑娘说她将和我只有一墙之隔

Song of the Graduation Season

On the grassy campus in the season of graduation
We wandered through the pagoda trees
My girl student hailed: "Professor, you are so beautiful
Let me capture this moment with a camera."

Something in the air
Made it so vague that the camera could hardly focus
The mist on the Miluo River is like the smog on the campus

Pondering for so long
Why Qu Yuan jumped into the river of tears
I finally understood History is a maiden's cheek
Did the exiled poet know
In 2000 years
Countries would have a fuzzy boundary
And so would be people's identity?

We passed that White building
Talking about how individuals shuttled in the
Flapping of history's banners

The maiden said
Her new campus will just be in the next block

但我知道
另一片大洋、另一个大陆
其实和一墙之隔的校园一样遥远

漫步到那两棵神奇的树旁
设计图纸曾被反复推翻
教学楼为他们而让路
他们有着500年的生命
知道一个秘密：
这是前身为坟场的一个校园
位于小西天、太平庄、铁狮子坟之间
总有赶不走的乌鸦会在校园里飞行

白色之楼下
绿草如茵 夕阳如血
孩子们在游玩

这是端午节前夜校园的漫步
我们凝望历史与当代
虚拟和现实
屈原与哈姆雷特
哈姆雷特与零落的花蕾
他们都一样深陷抑郁的泥潭
都走了、去了
留下诗句的

But I know
A next door neighbor will just be as a far
As the island in another ocean
We passed the two mysterious and legendary trees
Many designs were once discarded for them
And finally the classroom Complex yielded to the two trees
For they know a secret:
This campus was a graveyard
Many and many years ago
Located among the Little Western Paradise,
The Heavenly Peace Village and the Iron Lion's Graveyard
Crows always hover here and can't be driven away

On the grassy lawn by that White Building
Children were running and playing
The setting sun is bloody

We sauntered
On the eve of the Dragon Boat Festival
We mediated on the past and gazed at the present
The virtual and the real
Qu Yuan and Hamlet
Hamlet and the withered buds
All in the deep swamp of melancholy

还会在我们的脑海徘徊
但眺望明天时
我们必须以空杯心态

端午节后
就是你们的毕业典礼
我为你们写下过无数诗句
但你们的毕业照片上将没有我
因为我愿意做记忆的空白

2016.6

And all are gone
Still lingering in our memory
Are only those with a few poems
But looking into the future
We should empty our mind
Your commencement happens after the
Dragon Boat Festival
I have written unlimited poems for you
But on your graduation photograph
You will not find me
Because I choose to be blank in your memory

(Sheila and I took a walk on the campus. She took some pictures for me and I wrote this poem.)

白塔

我们向死而生
相聚时
已经种下分离的种子

天主教堂外的长椅上,
坐着泛神论 (pantheist) 的我和多神论 (polytheist) 的你
为了明天的分离
让我剪断我今天的黑发 给你
我要你许诺
如果你死去
留给我你的舍利

或者 如果我先离去
你为我修一座白色的塔
在那雪域高原
我 无人知晓
在你转经 转塔时
也许你会想起
很多年前
在汉地那个遥远的天主教堂
我曾剪断一段黑发 让你带去

2014.11

Pagoda

We live while facing death
When we met
The seeds of separation were already planted

On the bench
Outside the Cathedral
Sat you, the polytheist , and I, the pantheist
For tomorrow's farewell
Let me cut my long black hair for you
I bid you to promise
If you die first
Leave me your Buddha's relics, the pearls

If I die first
Build me a white pagoda
On the plateau of snow and white cloud
Where no one knows me
When you chant your prayers and circumambulate my white pagoda
Perhaps
You will remember
Many years ago
Outside a remote cathedral
I cut my long black hair
For you to take to the land of snow

尼泊尔

尼泊尔
我没有错过你
如果
我触摸过你、凝视过你、拥抱过你
我的心会更痛

尼泊尔
我终于明白
20 年前
他为什么放下一切 奔向你
奔向蓝毗尼

慈悲伟大的佛陀
让我像您一样
寂静平和地承受一切

尽管我又看见
尼泊尔的天空中
杜巴广场的微风里
有鸽子在飞翔

在世界屋脊的雪山之巅
苦修梵行的王子

Nepal

Nepal
I have never missed you
If I ever touched you, gazed at you and embraced you
My pang would be more unbearable

Nepal
It dawns upon me why
20 years ago
He abandoned all and ran to you
Ran to Lumbini

Great Compassionate Buddha
I'd follow you
Calmly and silently bear All

Though I see again
In the sky of Nepal
In the breeze of Durbar Square
Pigeons are fluttering

Over the snow-capped mountain
The Prince was meditating

是否已预知了今日的劫难
终将降于释迦族的子孙

慈悲伟大的王子
无法放下心中的牵挂
三次延缓血腥的琉璃王
然而王子
最终默然离去
寂静地承受释迦族的覆灭

我终于明白
他为什么奔向蓝比尼
20 年
他放下一切

尼泊尔
当雪山崩溃
古刹瓦解
我看见五蕴皆空
度一切苦厄的光明

尼泊尔
我总是忍不住回望你的美丽
然而回望，刹那之间
已成颠倒梦想

也许他
已经寂灭在你的废墟里

总有，流出来的眼泪
和没有流出来的泪
佛陀
让我像您一样
无畏无惧地将一切承受

2015.4

Did he already foresee the doom of the Shakyan clan
The earthquake?

The sentient Prince
Guided by the love at the bottom of his heart
Delayed the slaughter of Vidudabha king 3 times
Then resigned himself to the extinction of the Shakyan clan
It dawns upon me at long last
Why He ran to Lumbini
20 years ago, abandoning everything at hand.

Nepal
When the snow mountain collapsed
When the centuries-old monasteries crumpled
I saw the non-existence of everything
And the light that pacified all sufferings

Nepal
I can't help looking back at you, your beauty
But my retrospect has become delusion in a flash

Perhaps
He is already buried in your debris

There are always tears welling out
And tears swallowed in the eyes of
Great Compassionate Buddha
I'd follow you
And accept All without obscuration and with fear!

拉萨的天空下

行走在拉萨湛蓝的天空下
我在寻找永生的启示
膜拜于十二岁的释迦牟尼佛像前
我在渴求超越痛苦的灵丹妙药

是否得到
我并不知道

只知道
我得到了老上师最神圣的摸顶
和他最悲悯的慈爱

2018.4

Under the Sky of Lhasa

Under the water-blue sky of Lhasa
I trekked to seek the intimation of immortality
Prostrating to the statue of the 12 year old Buddha
I quested for the balm of my heart

Discovering it or not
I know not

Yet I have gained the Tibetan top-touch of my Lama Rinpoche
And his most precious compassionate love

在布达拉宫的翅膀下

西藏第一个神秘的夜晚
在布达拉宫的翅膀下
我遇见你

我栖息在圣城
在布达拉宫的翅膀下

你晒黑的脸发出微笑的光芒
召唤去圣城以西的地方

那一日，我跋涉后藏，
不为朝拜，只为追寻你的踪迹
那一午后，我在寺庙的深巷中穿寻
只为瞥见你难觅的踪影
那一路，我流太多的眼泪
只因为时光太短

在西藏的一个夜晚
我遇见了你
在布达拉宫的翅膀下
在那些被泪水浸泡的孤独夜晚里
我渴望的目光会在你的心海萦绕

2015.1

Beneath the Wings of Podala

I met you
My first night in Tibet

I dwelt in the Holy city
Beneath the wings of Bodala

Your suntanned beaming face
Summoned me to the southwest of Lhasa

That day, I went to Shigatse
Not for praying to gods, but to look for your traces
That afternoon, shuttling in the deep alleys of the monastery
Only to look for your red kasaya
That journey, I shed many tears
Only because the time I stayed with you was too short

My first night in Tibet
I met you
My wistful face will haunt you
All of my lonely nights beneath the wings of Bodala

外星人

来自外星的 Jack
我们在你的故乡相遇

我们在地球,我的家乡,相聚
可是这个星球不是你的故乡
Jack,我们终将分离

在城市的街头
With sweetness,Jack 你等着我
With calmness,Jack 你将我送别

Jack 你不是很懂我的星球
可是 Jack,你驱走了我的绝望
用你的戒律、慈悲

来自你故乡暴力的外星人
几乎将我强暴窒息
Jack,你是我的守护神
以你的出离心、慈悲心和戒律

多年以后
Jack 你已回到外星
我回望

在城市的街头,
我仍然看见你在等我
微笑、淡定、甜蜜

2015.1

Jack from another Star

Jack, you come from another planet
We met in your home star

We united on the earth, my hometown,
But this planet is not your home
Jack, we will separate one day

On the street of a city
With sweetness, Jack you wait for me
With calmness, Jack you separate with me

Jack you don't really understand the earth
But Jack, you have driven off my despair
With your commandments, with your compassion

The violent alien from your planet
Almost violated me and strangled me
Jack, you are my angel, you protected me
With your renunciation, compassion and commandment

After many years
Jack you will return to your home
When I look back
On the street of a city
I will still see you waiting for me
Smiling, calmly, with sweetness

念珠

在我燃烧、自焚成一把灰烬前
你回来了
在城市微弱的噪音里
你送给我一串佛珠
洁白 神圣 就像舍利子

这些神圣的珠子
散落在我胸前
夜晚在我心中作祟的欲望 化解了
黑暗中疯狂扼住我的焦虑 消散了

在咖啡的浓香里
你送给我一串白色的佛珠

我们走在冬天无雪的街头
圣洁的佛珠散落在我绛红色的披肩上
那颜色就让人想起 lama 的 Kasaya
就像拉萨的第一场雪
我的心中升起了宁静、平和
凝视着你眼眸深处
我与你分别

2015.1

Beads

Before I burn off and burn into a handful of ashes
You are back
In the faint noise of the city
You give me a string of white beads
Like the holy relics of Buddha's pearls

These holy beads scattered on my bosom
Yearnings haunting my heart like the rain at night dissolve
Anxieties holding me powerless in darkness clear off

In the scent of a café
You give me a string of holy beads

We walk on the street in deep winter
The holy beads adorn my deep red scarf evoking lama's kasaya
With tranquility and serenity arising in my heart
Like Lhasa's first snow
I look into your eyes
And see you off

我要带着一把剪刀来见你

我要带着一把剪刀来见你
因为你就要离去
我要剪下一缕头发给你
我们也许再也不能相见

我将要见到你
在千年的皇城墙外
昨夜的雪很小
Oh 雪 已成为传说中的神话
我穿越了无雪的冬天来见你

我沐浴 熏香
因为我将见到你
我们连指尖也不会相碰
不会握手 不会摸顶

我的头发
触及火花将化为灰烬
我带什么给你？
我的容颜
在你获得自由前 将会老去
留给你我的诗吧
它们已经开始流传

I'm Coming to You with a Pair of Scissors

I'm coming to you with a pair of scissors
Because that you are leaving
I will cut off a strand of hair for you
We might never meet again

I will meet you
outside the century-old imperial palace
Light was the snow last night
Which has soon passed into legend

I'm coming to you through the snowless winter
Bathed and perfumed
I am coming to you
Though there won't be handshake or Buddhist top-touch

Catching fire, my hair will turn to ashes
What can I give you?
My face will wither before your freedom is won
Let me leave you my poems
My lyrics have touched many hearts

我们在千年皇城外相聚
你将带我走过一片瓦砾般的胡同
那是我们的散步
然后
我们分别 你将继续被囚禁

在这个星球
你是个隐身人
为了见到我
为了在夜晚聆听我的声音
你现身 你登陆
每一次都是一场生命和自由的冒险

我穿过无雪的城市来见你
我跨越无量的海拔和你相聚
你将离去 离我更远
你的月亮会很清濯
我的月亮是一枚铜币

你走在前面
走在皇城墙外的瓦砾里
你说 这像你喜欢的乡村
你走在前面
我剪下一绺头发送你

我们一生的相聚
短过浮游的生命

我看着你眼眸深处
我们分别
可是你要我销毁所有关于你的诗句
因为你必须隐身
你的信仰弃绝思念与激情

我写给你的诗已经开始流传
我们就要永远分离

2015.2

We will meet outside the century-old imperial palace
Wandering through the old alleys
And sauntering amid the lanes
Then we part, you will be back to your bastille

You are an invisible alien being
To see me in the day, you appear
To hear me at night, you log on
But that is a hazard for you every time

I will cross the snowless city to see you
I have climbed the insurmountable altitudes to meet you
You are going, further away from me
Your moon will be water clear
My moon will be a copper coin

You will walk ahead of me amid lanes and debris
Outside the imperial palace
You once said, it was like the countryside
You walk fast, I lag behind
I hand you my hair just cut off
All our time together
Is shorter than the life of an ephemera

I look into your eyes when parting
You let me destroy and burn my poems for you
Because you must be invisible
Because your faith renounces passion and attachment

But my poems to you are already circulated
We part and we say goodbye

你的快乐

你快乐
为了驱散我的忧伤

你让我抹去你声音的刻录
你说你会为我录更多的声音

你说晚安
许诺明天会给我讲好多好多的故事

你总是让我相信
你会带我去很多地方

你微笑着
那样天真
我甚至忘记了你没有自由
我甚至忘记了悲伤
我与生俱来的阴影和诅咒

每一个深夜
我为你读诗

Your Happiness

Your happiness
Is to drive off my melancholia

You asked me to wipe off my saving of your voice
You said you would tally more for me when the time comes

You said good night
Promising you would tell me more stories tomorrow

You made me believe
You would take me to many places

You smiled
Innocently
I forget you don't have freedom
I forget sadness—my inborn shadow and curse

Every night
I read you poetry

我担心
我的诗会像海上女妖的歌
扰乱你的心
你就像荷马的奥德修斯
你不能追随你的情感
你只能在信仰的桅杆上把自己捆绑

唯有弃绝我的歌声
唯有弃绝聆听的快乐
你才能修行至臻
才能抵达你的彼岸

为了你
我不惧怕
失声和失语的静寂
为了你
我愿意寂灭

2015.2

I fear
My reading would tempt you
Like the Siren's songs
You are Homer's Odysseus
You can't follow your heart
Bound to the mast of your faith

Only by renouncing my songs
Only by renouncing your pleasure and desire
Can you have your spiritual ascetic practice
Can you reach the shore of Pure Land

For you
I don't fear aphonia and aphasia
For you
I don't fear the ultimate silence

我为你写诗

我为你写诗
那动荡的心境
郁结的愁绪
对未来的不期盼与期盼

我们站在山下
望着山顶白塔的剪影
还有半开的粉红的花蕾
你让我不要想未来,不要期盼
我说,好
可是,我的心,一直在郁结

你走了,白塔前景中的花蕾一定已经盛开
我想象着,想象着
可是,你已经到了异域的另一座山上
住在异域的空间

你的阳台上
已经没有了花朵
在那里
我们第一次相见
你说
你会种上花
就像夏天我们相见时一样

我从一开始就知道
我获得了你的爱
就像我已经获得了菩萨的祝福
可是
我们不能拥有未来
只能拥有过去和现在

2015.3

I Write Poems for You

I write poems for you
In turbulent moods
With melancholia that can't resolve
With expectation and non-expectation for the future

We stood at the foot of the hill
Looking up at the silhouette of the white pagoda
And the pink buds half in blossom
You asked me not to hope for the future, not to plan
I said yes
But my heart had been so sad

You left
The pink buds in the foreground of the pagoda
Must have blossomed
I envisioned, and I saw
But you are now in the mountain of another land
In the space of another territory

The flowers on your balcony
Have all withered
You say you will plant more
Like when we first met last summer

I knew from the beginning that
I have gained your love
As if I have gained the blessing of Bodhisattva
But we can't have the future
We can only have the past and the present time

最后一次见到你

最后一次见你
我哭了
你微笑,像一个孩子,没有忧愁焦虑
我知道
你珍惜我们在一起的时光
你知道你的微笑最能让我释然

你微笑
像一个孩子
你一直都是那样的
像那个长着翅膀的天使宝宝,我们的宝宝
然后
我们分别了
我这里,是一个没有雪的冬天
我猜想,你那里,是温暖潮湿的海边
你没有告诉我你将去哪里
我也不想知道

后来
我明白了分离的意义:涅槃寂灭

2014.12

The Last Time I Saw You

The Last time when I was with you
I cried, you smiled, like a child, without worry
I knew, you treasured the happiness of our time
You thought to smile is to comfort me

You were happy, like a child
You were always like that, like that smiling angel baby, our baby
Then we separated
I, here, a winter without snow
You, there, the warm, damp mist
I surmise you must be by the sea
You didn't tell me where you were going
And I didn't want to know

Since then
Separation's meaning is revealed to me: silence and nirvana

在郁金香的光泽中

在郁金香的光泽中
我穿越故都的花粉和柳絮
重新见到你

在城市心脏的悸动中
我们啜饮着各自的咖啡
扑鼻而来的
是你永远散发着的寺院气息
久别重逢的内容
是一起念诵咒语

仍然惊惧昨夜冰雹的残痕
忧伤着未来的不可避免性
我祈求你再教给我一点或更多
因为我已经得到佛的准许

春风中的一对对情侣
亲密相依 不可分离
在时光的滤镜下
他们单薄 赤裸 脆弱

我和你
正襟危坐

昂首而行
隔着戒律的距离
在车站
我们再次告别

记得
饮完咖啡时
我送给你
我的那块提拉米苏和巧克力

2018.4

In the Aura of Tulips

In the aura of tulips
Crossing the pollen and the willow catkin in the air
I met you again in the ancient capital

In the throbbing of the city's heart
We sipped each other's coffee
Yet greeting me is your monastery's aromas
After long parting
We chanted mantra for reunion

Still haunted by the memory of last night's hailstorm
Sad for the future's inevitability
I solicited you to teach me more, one bit more
For I have gained the Buddha's permission

In the breeze of Spring,
Lovers intimately huddled together, so inseparable
But in Time's lenses
They are naked and fragile

You and I
Seriously sat in the cafe
And solemnly walked on the street
Seperated by Commandment
At the station
We said farewell

Still remember
When drinking off the coffee
I gave you my Tiramisu, my favorite dessert

致信仰

在生死汹涌如波涛的山坡上
我听见痛苦的呻吟、愤怒的喊叫、谵妄的呓语
我只能忆念你

在被病痛的苦海湮没的黑夜里
在充斥着死亡之歌的雨声中
我梦见你

在太阳下,我目睹惨烈恐怖的鲜血
在我的怀里,我的父亲睡去
我流着眼泪为他唱着摇篮曲

就这样
我涉过苦海
靠着对你的忆念
靠着想念对你的想念
我涉过死亡涌动的苦海
尽管没有你的消息
我仍然向往你

For Faith

In the mountain where life and death surge like waves
I heard the incessant painful moans, angry yellings
And delirious ravings
Nothing I could do but to think of you

In the sea of sufferings at dark night
In the sound of the falling rain where death's carols pierced
I dreamed of you

Under the sun
I saw the heartrending ghastly blood
In my arms, my father fell into sleep
I cried, singing him a lullaby

So it was
I trekked in sorrow
By means of remembering you
I tossed in the sea of pain
By means of remebering my memories of you
Where death was lurking everywhere
Without any news from afar
I still yearned for you

告诉你或不告诉你

我是否应该告诉你
这棵树开满了粉色的花
虽然雾霾深重

我是否可以告诉你
花正在凋落
虽然天空晴朗

在另一个地方
其实
你和我过着同样的生活
每天
重复着同样的内容

当夏天来临时
我是否可以告诉你
花全退了
树全绿了

我不愿在温暖的春风中
想起冬天的寒冷和萧瑟

太阳底下
没有什么新鲜事
你知道或不知道
让你知道或不让你知道
太阳底下
都一样

背靠群山的你
将看见我
在粉色细碎的繁花中想念你
在阵阵的花瓣雨中忘却你

To Tell You or not

This tree is in full pink blossom
Regardless of the deep smog

To tell you or not
The flowers have withered
Despite that the sky is clear

In another place
You live the same life as mine
Everyday
Repeating the same routine

When summer comes
Whether can I tell you
The flowers are gone
The tree is deep green

I don't want to think of winter's coldness and desolation
In spring's breeze

Under the sun
Nothing is new
Whether you know or know not
To let you know or not to let you know
Under the sun
All are the same

With mountains outside your window
You will see me
Standing under the pink and tiny blossoming flowers
Missing you
Bathing in the rain of petals
Forgetting you

写在母亲节

五月的这一天
空气中飘散着玫瑰和紫丁香的芬芳
路上撒满了槐树和榆树浅色的花瓣

关于母亲的记忆
纷沓而至 潮水般涌来
啊，那些已逝去的母亲
那些依然健在的母亲
感恩，悲伤——
我们席卷在情感的流沙中
感动，疲惫，哀怨

女儿在远离故土的山巅
俯瞰雨中苍老的世界
郁郁寡欢

突然
乌云消散 阳光普照
窗户都变为金黄色
道路都晶亮清澈
一道彩虹贯穿天空

突然忆起
前世今生的所有母亲
奇迹突然到来
今天是妈妈的节日
五月的第二个星期天

2017.5

On Mother's Day

One day in May
The air is full of the fragrance of roses and lilacs
The road is strewn with
The petals of pagoda trees and elm trees

Memories about mothers alive and gone
Surge like waves
We are lost in the quicksand
Of gratitude and sentiments
Touched, weary and melancholic

On top of a mountain far way from her mother
The daughter is overlooking the tired and aged world
Feeling sad

Suddenly
The dark clouds disperse
The golden light shines
Upon the transparent windows and bright road
The rainbow crosses the sky

With the influx remembrances
Of all the mothers in our past life and present life
The miracle arrives
On the Mother's Day
The second Sunday of in the 5th month

五月的多伦多

穿越 15 个光年
她来到多伦多寻找他
想着 Jacksonville 绿草如茵的墓园
阳光灿烂,佛罗里达

在多伦多五月透明的微风中
她看见无数蓝色的眼睛
但都没有他眼里的大海那样蔚蓝
她独自行走在多伦多街头
为了和他的灵魂对话
为了怀念
他曾说
她的眼里总有光芒闪烁
尽管她总是焦虑不断

在五月将尽的多伦多
他应该看见
有持戒者在窗前为他写诗
她依然是小小的
昔日的执念妄想
已变为舍弃一切的坚韧、勇敢

Toronto in May

Traversing 15 light years
She came to Toronto for him
Reminiscent of the green graveyard in Jacksonville and the sunlit Florida

In the transparent breeze of May
She saw many blue eyes
But none is bluer than the sea of his eyes
She walked lonely on the streets of Toronto
To talk to his soul in nostalgia

He once said
Her eyes were always shimmering
Though laden with anxiety

Toward the end of May in Toronto
He should see a precept observer
Writing him a poem by the window
Small as she remains
Her passion has turned into resilience and courage

那一年三月的多伦多
他忘记携带娑婆世界中他的标签
只带着陆地行驶的通行证
在空中穿行而来
而她踩着碧空的波浪而到
为了文学虚拟的世界

可是空性弥漫一切
这世间唯一的真理
就是缘起性空

他总说
她的眼中有天才之光在闪烁
即使她充满焦虑 偏执 妄念

在多伦多三月的街头
他说：
如果蓝色的大海
配上棕色的沙滩
该多美
那时，她狂野又反叛

越过15个光年
她已经成为智者和勇士
但再也没有更湛蓝的大海

That March in Toronto
He left his passport somewhere
And flew to Toronto with his driving license
While she walked through the waves in the sky
Both in pursuit of the fictional world of literature

But emptiness permeated
And the only truth in this world results from the emptiness of nature

He used to say
Lights of talent were shining in her eyes
Even though she was anxious and manic

On the street of Toronto in March
He said:
If only the blue sea was framed with brown shore
Back then
She was wild and rebellious

15 light years later,
She was now wiser and braver
But she found no bluer sea, purer sail and straighter mast

更笔直的桅杆
更洁白的风帆
她独自奔赴多伦多
因为她不能去佛罗里达的墓园
他的身边

多伦多的天空
没有压抑她的苍白
总有颜色和云彩
这里黑夜很短 光的时辰很长

在他走后
他对她所有的期望都将实现
五月将尽的多伦多 天空蔚蓝
白云有时会染上大海的颜色
安大略湖广阔如大海
他的灵魂伴着她散步在湖畔

她独自坐在窗前
凝望多伦多天空的蔚蓝
看云彩像白色的海浪在移动
倾听暮色中大提琴的哭泣

她将再次在碧空中踏浪而归
像一只孤独的鸟儿

在思念之中独自来去
而多伦多的天空中
没有留下任何痕迹

She ran to Toronto alone
Because she couldn't pay homage to his tomb in Florida

The sky of Toronto set off her pale
With its azure sky and white clouds
The night is so short and the day so long

When he is gone
All his wishes for her would come true
The sky was as azure as the ocean in late May

She sat in front of the window, lonely
Gazing at the blue sky:
white clouds walking like white waves
While the cello wept in the twilight

Her trip back would be as lonely as her trip here
She flew like a lonesome bird
Leaving no trace in the sky of Toronto

在那拉提的草原上

生命的最后
只是短暂的回望

为那一朵白色的小花
我洒下叹息

在那拉提草原那一朵白色的毡房前
我看见你从野花中摇摆地走来
我抱起了你
和你肌肤相亲
紧贴着你稚嫩温软的脸颊
你的奶香将我心中的冰雪融化

在神秘的湖光中
喀纳斯山巅那朵孑然一身的白色小花
向着那拉提草原眺望
她看见我从野花中抱起了你
脸上流溢着灿烂的光芒

哈萨克的小宝宝
在南疆梦魇般的荒漠里
在炙热的戈壁滩上
我又看见

On Nalati's Grassland

The last moment of life
Would be just an overlook of the track

For that little white flower
I cast a sigh

In front of the white Yurt
On Nalati's grassland
I saw you toddling to me amid flowers
I picked you up
And held you in my arms
Nestling against your tender soft face
Your breath reminding me a mother's breast
Melting the ice in my heart

In the mysterious shimmering of Lake Kanas
The lonely white lower on top of the mountain
Overlooked Nalati's grassland
And saw me clasping you to my bosom
My face beaming with light

My Kazakhstan Toddler
In the eerie and sizzling Gobi of southern Xinjiang
My mind's eye saw you again

在草原上，在青松下
在毡房前，从野花中
在流水旁
你摇摆着向我走来
我看见自己抱起了你
紧贴着你柔软稚嫩的脸颊

这被定格的一刻
便是一个女人最浪漫
最贞洁、最动人的梦想

生命的最后
只是短暂的定格和回望
我的哈萨克小宝宝
我看见你走来
从那拉提的草原上

2016.8

On the grassland, under the pine
In front the white Yurt, and by the river side
Where flowers grew
You walked to me unsteadily
I saw myself taking you in my arms
Nestling against your tender face
Skin on skin

This captured moment
Is the most touching
And the most chaste dream of a romantic woman

The last moment of life
Would be just a overlook of the track
A framed instance in the mind's eye
My little Kazakhstan Toddler
My little baby walking to me
On Nalati's grassland

半地下室的春天

我的窗户只有一半在地面以上
我只能看见匆匆行走的脚
我只能想象着记忆中行走者的脸

我的春天
是照片上一片浸染的蓝天
前景中的树和冬天的记忆一样灰黑
可是干枯的枝丫上粉白的花蕾已经开满

我的心穿梭在
地铁黑暗的隧道
但我心灵的眼睛
凝望着离太阳最近的部落
金光闪闪的寺庙、白云和蓝天

我看不见
窗外枯树长出的粉白花蕾
因为我的窗户太低矮
我在阴冷的小房间里
读着一本凄楚的书
在书页的空白处
记下我流动的思绪
就像书中

My Spring

Only the upper half of my window is above the ground
The only sight is the roving feet
Only I can imagine the expression of the travellers

My spring
Is a patch of blue sea in the sky of my photo
The tree in the foreground still appears grey and black
Like winter's memory
But the pink buds are already sprouting
On its dark and barren branches

I am a mental traveller in dark tunnels
But my mind's eye
Gazes at the tribe closest to the sun
Its golden temples, white cloud and blue sky

I can't see
The pink buds sprouting on the dark barren branches
Because my window is half buried.
In my dim and chilly cellar
I am reading a lonely book
In its margin
I write down my flowing thoughts

山洞里那个孤独的受伤女人
点燃了有限的蜡烛
依靠着刻满历史和文明的洞壁
在历史书的空白处
写下她最后的字

我生活在很小的地方
我的窗户看不见天空
只能看见偶尔走过的人们的脚
可是
我的春天已经到来

2016.4

As the solitary wounded woman in the Swimmer's Cave
Lighted her last kindle
Against the mural where history and civilization were inscribed
She wrote her last words
In the blank page of her history book

I live in a small place of liminality
My window has no sky
I can only see the roving feet of some people
Yet
My spring comes

在城市的掩护下

城市纵横的大街小巷和密集的人群
很容易掩护一切
我遇见了你
但我们彼此隐匿
直到在一个深夜你唤醒我
告诉了我一个梦幻的真实
它只存在于你阈限的空间

在孤独中
我思考这个真实的梦幻
想象与不安升起

一首潜在的抒情诗在那里
我们是否应该把它变长、变深、
扩充为小说或剧本?
你知道一切都会过去
我也知道

所以
我选择聆听你在阈限状态下的独白
看抒情诗如何变为小说和剧本
如何被戏剧化地演出

而我们静静地在城市的两端
隔空观看着演出中的自己

2016.3

Under the Cover of City

Under the cover of city's network of streets and alleys
And its vast population, deception is easy
I met you and we were deceived
Until one night you called telling me a half truth
Which only existed in your limbo and torpor
I pursued it in my loneliness and restlessness arises

The potential lyric is there
Should we make it theatricalized under the deception of a city
You know all will pass
And I know it too

So I choose to listen to you speaking in your limbo
And all is cast and staged
And we only watch ourselves
In the sky of the city respectively

藏地的小女孩

藏地的小女孩
纯真的笑靥
打动了汉地冰雪般的少女
寺院里来了高贵的客人
她会为他们展现
东方最精湛的茶艺
并弹奏古琴一曲

白石崖的法语梵音中
奇妙的光晕下
冰雪少女的镜头对准了
藏地小女孩春花般的小脸
小女孩的阿妈正忙于嗷嗷待哺的弟弟
阿爸正磕长头膜拜

雪山之巅
金色的寺庙旁
藏族小女孩稚嫩的脸颊
将来自汉地冰雪少女的母性唤醒

The Little Tibetan Girl

The innocent smile on the face of
The little Tibetan girl
Softened the heart of the Han maiden
Who was as pure as ice and snow
When distinguished guests arrived at the monastery
The Han maiden would entertain them
With the best tea ceremony in the east
And play an ancient seven-stringed musical instrument

In Lama Rinpoche's prayers at the White Rock Cliff
Under the mysterious halo
The Han maiden's camera focused
On the smiling face of the Tibetan girl
Whose mother was breast feeding the crying younger brother
While the father was prostrating in front of Buddha

On the top of the snow-capped mountain
Outside the golden temple
The puerile and tender face of the little Tibetan girl
Awakened the motherhood
Of the maid from the Han land

她如何才能守身如玉
且不借助现代医学科技
却又能孕育生命的奇迹
她凝视着藏地的小女孩
并将她一揽入怀
像妈妈，像姐姐

在老上师的祈福声中
白石崖天降祥瑞
少女的心中播下了母性的种子
如同在大地的土壤里播下秘密

2015.6

How could she conceive the miracle of life
While remaining chaste
And refraining from modern medical technology
She gazed on the little Tibetan girl
And held her in her arms

In the prayers of the beloved Lama Rinpoche
Auspicious signs appeared in the sky above the White Rock Cliff
Just like a miraculous seed in the soil
The seed of motherhood was buried in the heart of the maid

送别

我跨越了十年的时光
来到地铁站等你

十年前那个夏天的上午
我如何能看到这个三月最后一天的黄昏

人群中 这些面孔
幽灵一般显现
湿漉漉的黑色枝条上的许多花瓣

我看见你带着僧侣般的戒律
思想家的专注和一种心在别处的神情
穿过时光黑色的隧道
站在扶梯上走过来

我们当时谈过的
连你都认为最可怕的人生痛苦
我已经静静地经历过
看见你走过来
我嘴角翕动
可是最终还是没能告诉你

在黑暗中
在时光的隧道里 我送走你
看着你的背影消失
我这才明白
这一生你脸上都有的肃穆神情
无法融入当下的痛苦
和心不在焉的孤寂

2016.3

Seeing You off

I stepped over 10 light years
To wait for you in a metro station

On that summer morning 10 years ago
How could I envision this last day's twilight in March

The apparition of these faces in the crowd
Petals on a wet black bough

I saw you
Shuttling in the dark tunnel
On the escalator
Carrying with you the commandments of a monk
The look of a thinker's concentration
And your mind is always absent

I have silently undergone
The sorrows which even you regarded as unbearable 10 years ago
When I see you coming
My lips are trembling
Yet I fail to tell you what have happened to me all these years

In darkness
In the tunnel of light
I send you off
Seeing you disappear
I finally understand
The solemn look you have whole of your life
And your pain of
Being unable to get merged into the present reality

静坐

世间无所畏惧的人们
你们不知道
在绿色的寺庙里
男人们为何面壁静坐

世间不懂受戒和守戒的人们
你们不懂何为净戒和净行
你们不懂为何她在雨中送走他
为何没有握他的手
没有附身拥抱正在停车的他
没有让自己凝望幽暗中他的面庞

在不可穿透的雾霾里
心中有着一阵酸楚
净戒的力量仿佛无情
让他没有迟延地离去
回到他该去的地方

为的是让他达到终点前
少走一条不必走的岔路
为了在冬日的午后
教堂的乐声不会让
静坐在那里的他受伤

2016.11

Meditating

Fearless people in the world
You don't know
Why men in the green mosque
Sit silently before the wall

People in the world
You don't understand Buddhist Initiation and abstinence
You don't' understand
Why she didn't hold his hands when sending him off in the drizzle
With no hugging, without looking at his silhouette in dim light

In the impenetrable mists
Poignancy arises in her heart
The power of clean abstinence is cruel
Letting him leave without tarrying
Letting him go back to where he belongs

Let him take one less diverged road
Before he reaches his destination
And in that winter afternoon
When he sits in the cathedral
The rising hefty music
Will not cut a heavenly scar in his heart

失去父亲的女儿

失去父亲的女儿
将继续生活
永远面临无语的大海
永远眺望那未知的海岸

失去父亲的女儿
将永远生活在对父亲的记忆中
却又不能让那记忆将自己掩埋

行走在世界尽头的草原上
眺望北极最北的冰山之巅
远方的父亲
你是女儿心中不舍的牵挂
女儿要回到你的身边
陪伴你到生命最后一息
可是你要女儿
继续她的旅途
不要因为你而停顿
哪怕很短暂

A Fatherless Daughter

A daughter deprived of her father
Will continue to live
She will face the silent sea
Overlooking that unknown side

The daughter deprived of her father
Will live in memory of her Father
But can't let herself get drowned in memory's tide

Walking in the Northern prairie of the West
Looking down on the top of Mount Kanas
Father in the distance
You are always in your daughter's mind
She must come back to you
In your last hour
But you wanted her to
Continue with her journey
With no stop
Even for you, even for a moment

女儿没有错过
生命中每一处美丽的风景
可是她
最后还是不顾一切地奔赴你的身边
在你最后的一刻
将你拥抱入怀

父女前世就有着不舍的爱恋
于是有了后世的相聚和不舍的相依
但他们依然面临不可阻挡的生离死别

女儿拥抱着溘然长眠的父亲
然后亲手将他掩埋
前世的后世就是今生
让他们后世再做一次父女
让他们来世再一次深深相爱

2016.10

Your daughter didn't miss
Any beautiful scenery in her life
But she
Ran to you despite of all
In your last moment
To Hold you in her arms and cried

There was inseverable attachment in their past life
Between a father and his daughter
Hence their meeting, loving and tarrying
Yet their parting was inevitable

The daughter in her arms
Held her father who was in long sleep
And buried him with her own hands
The past's future is the present
Let them again be father and daughter
Let them love again in their afterlife

我的燃灯节

我历尽了多少苦难
才与你们相遇
我经过了多少苦难
才与你们相聚
恒河中有多少沙粒
每一粒沙都是一颗心,一个世界
要历尽多少修炼
一粒砂才能进入另一粒沙的世界

如果我在苦难中死去
我将见不到你们
如果我在苦难中麻木
即使见到你们
我将无法报以微笑
我将无法融入你们的世界

和你们相遇前
我已经磕长头匍匐山路
和你们相聚前
我已经学习你们的文字、像画
阿克和阿尼说
你们的文字来自梵文
学习它,会得到无量的加持

My Butter Lamp Day

How many sorrows must I go through
Before I can finally meet you?
How many sufferings must I undergo
Before I can ultimately unite with you?
How many grains of sand are there in the Ganges river?
Every sand grain is a heart and a world
How many trials must be required
Before one sand grain can enter into another?

If I die in sorrow
I would not meet you
If I become numb in suffering
Even if I meet you
I would not have shimmering soft smile
And would not melt into your world

Before meeting you
I have prostrated on the mountain road in the highland of snow
Before uniting with you
I have studied your language, which looks like drawings
Monks say
Your language derives from Sanskrit
Studying it, one will be immeasurably blessed

在这个浮华的世界
有人不会嘲笑我简朴
在雾霾中
有人和我一起点灯
在这个校园
师生只有课堂上才相识
课下即为陌路
我遇见一个来自雪域高原的小女孩
她长着和我一样深深的眼睛
第一次见到我
她就对我说
我和她过去曾相见

相聚前
已经有很多因缘
相聚时
我噙着眼泪
那一夜
烛光一直在闪烁
我看见自己和你们在一起
微笑合十
祈祷膜拜

过去心不可得
现在心不可得
未来心不可得
我应达到事过即灭的境界
可是第二天
雾霾的级别又是红色警报
我注视自己的内心
我看见燃灯节的烛光汇聚成海洋
还在闪烁
我还和你们在黑暗中合十膜拜

2016.12

Despite the vanity of the world
Someone would never laugh at my simplicity
In smog
Someone would light the lamps with me
On the campus where professors and students
Become strangers right after class
I met a girl from the highland of snow
Who has eyes as deep as mine
Though she first met me,
She said she had met me before

Before we met
Our Karmas were already there
When we united
My eyes were wet
That night
The butter lamps were shimmering
I saw myself smiling with you
Past thoughts are intangible
So are present thoughts and future thoughts
I should let things go once they happened

But the next day
The smog reached the level of red alert
I looked into my heart
Still seeing us praying together with hands in namaste
Still seeing the sea of butter lamps flickering

我是冲动的风

我如此冲动
我是你生命中的一阵风

我是自由的风
这一世
你每一夜都会独自在床上
感觉我看不见的抚摸
听我的哭泣和呼唤
有我敲击你窗户的夜晚
你将无法入睡

这一世
你注定贞洁始终
然而你羡慕又惧怕
我的冲动、自由和执着

2017.6

I am the Wind, so Impulsive

So impulsive
I entered your life like a gust of wind
Free is the wind
Which fumbled you every night
When you are in a lonely bed
The touch, however, went unnoticed
Sobbing and crying
I knocked so hard on your window
That you could hardly fall asleep

In this life
You are destined to be chaste from beginning to end
Yet you admire and fear
My impulse, audacity and freedom

我是一名来自内地的小孩

我是一名来自内地的小孩
我来自死人埋葬死人的地方
人类历史上最悲惨的地震
有一天 我看见了海
我发现了美和恐惧
但如果你要我忘记海草与海马
我就将他们抹去

孤独是你给我唯一的馈赠
你让我成为一名诗人

2008.12

I am an Child from the Inland

I am an inland child
I come from a land where the dead bury the dead
The most tragic earthshake in human history
I saw the sea one day
I find beauty and terror
But if you wanted me to forget the sea weeds and the sea horse
My mind will erase them for you
Solitary prowess is the only gift you give me
And you made me a poet

饮茶时光
——写给哈罗德·布鲁姆

看不见的黑暗河流升起又沉落
当我们在一起饮茶,品尝着您的无花果

在一座有着一万五千册书籍的房子里
白天和夜晚一样寂静
有一天,可能不会太远
书会消失,房子会倒下

那一天已经被预见
当我们啜饮着茶,品尝着您的无花果

一次晚启的航程,一次焦虑的追寻
为了找到一个隐喻
描写一条黑暗的河流
有着堤岸和水坝
流在我们各自的心中

直到有一天
我们一起坐下
正如您所想象的
您想象和预见到了一切
直到有一天

Tea Time
  ——for Harold Bloom

The unseen dark river rises and falls
As we drink tea and taste your figs

In a house which has more than 15,000 books
A day can be as quiet as night
One day, which might not be very far
The books will be gone
And the house will collapse

That day is being envisioned
As we drink tea and taste your figs

A belated quest, and an anxious one
To find a trope
For a dark drive, banked and dammed
In each individual

Until one day we sit together
As you have imagined
You have imagined everything
And you have already foreseen all
Until the day when we have tea quietly
Only you and me
I know it is a River, running in each other's heart

我们安静地坐在一起饮茶
只有您和我
我知道那是一条河
留在我们各自的心中

摸着杯子的手
被时光挫败的手

一个没有女儿的父亲的悲哀
一个羽翼未丰的诗人的探寻
一个没有父亲的学生的焦虑

放着两只茶杯的实木桌子
就像教室里放着书的课桌
我们坐在各自的椅子里
饮着自己的茶
就像在上课

我们凝视着真正的自己
这是我一生中最安静的饮茶时光
最有魅力和最悲哀的一次

多么阈限,多么完整
我用一只瓦缸喝茶的体验
被一只颤抖的手挑中的瓦缸

Hands groping for mugs
Hands defeated by time

The sadness of a daughterless father
The quest of a fledgling poet
And the anxiety of a fatherless pupil

The wood table where two mugs stand
Resembles the one in the classroom where books lie
We sit in each other's chair, having tea
Like having our class

We see each other as we truly behave
The quietest tea in my life
The quietest talk, and the most charming one
The saddest one too

How limited, but how complete
Is my experience of having tea
In a mug, chosen by a trembling hand

在饮茶的时光
业力暂时躲避
命运也隐退瞬间
但不能被避免
最后的失落终究无法逃脱

我们饮着茶,品尝着您的无花果
静观黑暗河流的起落
我们看见了堤岸和水坝
以及洪峰的危险

奇迹不是为我们产生
正如树叶不属于冬天
因为已经是结束的终点

所以
我们静静地啜饮着茶
然后说再见

2006.4

In tea time
Destiny is shunned for a while
And doom dodged
But there is no way to prevent Doom
To ward off the ultimate disappointment

We drink tea and taste your figs
As the dark river rises and falls
We see the bank and the dam
And the danger of deluge

Miracle is not meant for us
As leaves are not winter's because it is the end

Therefore
We have our tea quietly, and we say goodbye

让我

让我带着沧桑和你站在一起
让细细的皱纹爬上我的脸颊
让我枕着海浪孤独地入睡
让我听你说
幼年的你如何渴望到达有灯的地方

让我在海浪声中禅定冥想
让我的宁静和戒律感染你
当你游戏如蝴蝶在花间翻飞
让我浅浅的愁绪
能唤起你今生对信仰的渴望
去一个黑夜里有灯的地方

2017.5

Let Me——

Let me stand by you with a touch of life's vicissitudes
Let the fine wrinkles crawl on my face
Let me fall into sleep on the pillow of lonely waves
Let me hear you saying:
How that country lad yearn for a place of light

Let me enter into transcendental meditation
In the low sounds of the lapping waves
Let my serenity and precepts touch you
While watching you afar fluttering around like a butterfly
Let my subtle sadness
Awaken your yearning for faith
And a well-lighted place

给胡建

记得那一年夏天,认识了你
很快我们分离
在帝都地铁高峰的中转处
你拥抱了我
那时的我
如沉木一般
深深地陷在四季的沼泽里
但毕竟还有记忆

时光穿梭
我在空港的暮色中
看见你探出窗户拍摄
雨中滨海城市的夜景
原来你在那里等我
于是,我说走就走的旅程
不再孤寂

你想为我拔下一根白色的丝线
但怕弄疼我,又放弃

在雨中
你拥抱我
我要去海上的小岛朝拜
而两个羽翼洁白的天使在海的对面等你

你送我一把檀香木梳
在微笑和闪烁的泪光中
我们再一次分离

2016.5

我们相遇在
海边离渡母岛很近的小城
在滨海的迷雾里
我们欢笑着,就像没有忧愁的少女
赤足在浪花里奔跑

Dearest

I met you that summer
Soon we departed
The rush hour of the subway
Witnessed your embrace of me
A lady in the swamp of melancholy, like a log
Incapable of articulation whatsoever

The shuttle of time brings me back to
The dusk at the airport
I saw your upper part hanging out of a window
Capturing the drizzling night of the coastal a city with your camera
Oh, you were waiting for me
My spontaneous and wayward trip
Was no longer solitary

We met
In the city by the sea
Amid the mist on the beach
We laughed and Ran in the breakers, barefoot,
Like two maidens, so carefree
You tried in vain to pull off a silk thread for me
Fearing it might hurt

In the light drizzle
You hugged me
Before my pilgrimage
To the Island of Bodhisattva
While two seraphs were
Waiting for you
On the other side of the sea

You gave me a comb of sandalwood
With smile and shimmering tears
We departed again

写在情人节

我听见铁锹铲去积雪的声音
在冬日明亮的光线里,
在积雪透亮的空气中

我听见铁锹在阳光下铲着积雪
铲去了昨夜我在心中为你洒下的叹息

啊,我那焦虑的暴风雨之夜
当天空落下雪片
我的心也洒下叹息

在应该忆念圣人圣瓦伦丁的这一天
我听见邻居的铁锹铲着白雪
也铲去了我心中铭刻的你的名字
落雪所雕刻的叹息
在暴风雪的夜晚冻结

我听见铁锹的节奏和音乐
在冬日明亮的午后

2006.2

On Valentine's Day

I heard the music of a spade shoveling snow
In the bright light and clear sky of a winter day

I heard snow shoveling in the sunlight
Shoveling the sighs, too, I dropped for you last night

Ah, my night of anxiety in the blizzard
When the sky dropped flakes
My heart dropped sighs
Sighs for you
A bosom friend so far away

On the day to remember Saint Valentine
I heard the music of neighbor shoveling snow
Shoveling your name carved in my sighs, too
Sighs carved and frozen on the night of the blizzard

I heard the spade's resounding melody
On a bright winter afternoon

在瓦尔登湖为你挑选的明信片

记得那一年深冬
去康科德旅游
我为你挑选了一张明信片
在结冰的瓦尔登湖面
在明信片上
写着纳撒尼尔·霍桑的诗句
那是我喜欢的一首诗
我想在你生日时将它寄给你
但我不知道你的生日
我也不敢问
这小小的明信片
像雪花般孤独
我的心犹豫着陷入了静寂
知道这张孤独的明信片将伴随着我
知道有一天它会丢失

明信片消失在
我的那些书中
二月已经过去

我又面临搬迁
为了开始新的生活
或者,为了回到过去的生活

Choosing a Postcard for You in Concord

When I took the Concord trip in the depth of winter,
I bought you a postcard on the icy Walden Pond,
On the card was a lyric by Nathaniel Hawthorn
The beloved lyric was actually
Hester Prynne's soliloquy in *The Scarlet Letter*
I was thinking of posting it to you in your birth month
I, however, had no idea of your birth date
Nor do I have the heart to ask you about it
Or to startle you, with this slim postcard
As forlorn as a snowflake
Silence and hesitation reigned my heart
I knew the lonely birthday card would keep me company alone
Until it gets lost one day in the future

It got lost in the books I bought and borrowed
And February has long passed

One day when I move again for a new life
Or, just go back to my old life

当我整理书籍和手稿时
或者孤独地阅读时
这张瓦尔登湖明信片
将飘落在地

我将附身将它拾起
想起你
想起多年前的康科德之行
想起我如何在安静的小小纪念馆里
为你挑选了这张明信片
霍桑的家就在不远处
当我将亨利·大卫·梭罗孤独的墓碑握在我手心时
我给你的明信片正躺在斜挎在我肩上的黑色书包里

2006.4

When I am packing my books and my manuscripts
Or when I am reading in solitude as I always am
That Walden Pond postcard I bought for you
Will drop onto the floor

And I will bend down to pick it up
Thinking of you, and my Concord trip,
And how I bought it at the quiet small museum
Near the home of Nathaniel Hawthorn
And When I held in my hand
The lonely tomb stone of David Henry Thoreau
And how the postcard I bought for you was
In my black school bag, hanging on my shoulder

That day, when the lost postcard drops onto the floor
Will be many years away
Many years after this year when I write you so many poems

枫树

你是否记得枫树
在明亮的日光中
你开车带着我驶向大瀑布

当春天到来时,你说,
枫叶会杂染天空

你是否记得枫树
当你夜里驱车带着我
为我购买由枫叶提炼的糖果

我已经回来
和你相隔万水千山

踯躅在博物馆的一幅油画前
在幻灯片的背景中
我又见枫叶

从那以后
你就像浪涛
常常拍击我心海的堤岸
带着飘落的枫叶

这里的香山
生长着无数枫树
但和加拿大的不同

2005.3

Maple Trees

Do you still remember the maple trees
In bright daylight
You drove me to Niagara

When spring comes, you said,
The maple leaves would dye the sky
Miscellaneously and splendidly

Do you still remember the maple trees?
And the night When you drove me
To a supermarket
For sweets
made from maples

I have come back
So far away from you
Watching a painting in a museum
Against the backdrop of a lantern slide
Maple leaves bounced into my sight

It is you

Ever since then
You have been in my heart
Associated in my memory with
Maple trees

Indeed the Fragrant Hill abounds in maple trees
They, however, are so different from
Those in Canada

当郊外的栀子花盛开时

当郊外的栀子花盛开时
我见到你
想起了我爱的他

那些透明的夏日夜晚
我摘下一条树枝,带着花蕾

孤独的花
孤独的女人走到了人群前
为了你

每一次走过你的窗前
我都找寻你

我踯躅　徘徊
在你的窗前　在你的门外
我离你如此之近

但是你的心
如此熟悉而温柔的心
我却无法知晓

我看见你和他们一起漫步,

When Gardenia Flowers Bloomed in the Suburb

When the suburban Gardenia flowers bloomed
The sight of you
Reminded me of my previous love

Those transparent summer nights
I plucked a twig with budding flowers

Solitary were the flowers
So was the lady who braved the crowd for you

Every time passing by your window, I looked for you

I lingered and wandered in hesitation
Outside your window, outside your door
I felt so close to you

But your heart
Familiar and tender heart
Still mysterious to me

I saw you wandering with them

在那个阴影密布的透明夜晚，
还有一个世俗的仙女

我在路上，在微风中
在那个透明的夜晚
我知道我已完全遁入自己的世界
一个孤独的隐士

我看见你远去
消失在深绿色的叶间
我的心痛苦地下坠
我只能等到明天才能见到你
我忧郁的被泪水浸泡的夜晚

在夏夜透明的微风中
我等你
心中充满了喜悦和孤独
在孤独中，我走过你的窗前

我们需要沉默
因为栀子花早已凋谢
我摘下树枝
栀子花就在我手中

栀子花已经从树枝上坠落了

在拂晓之前它将凋落
我手中这伤痕累累的花朵啊
在夏夜的微风中它将为你而凋落
你为何视而不见

2005.12

On that shadowy and transparent night and with a mundane nymph
As I stood on the road in the breeze
I knew I had retired into seclusion, recoiling into a solitary self
As I watched you fading into the depth of green leaves
My heart sank
I could not see you until tomorrow
After a night, tearful and melancholy

In the breeze of the cold transparent summer night
I waited for you
Full of joy and solitude
I passed your door in silence

We were desperate for silence
As the gardenia flowers had long withered
On the twig I plucked
Pity is the flower in my hand

The gardenia flower had
Fallen from the twig
They would die before the dawn light broke
This bruised flower in my hand
Would die for you in the breeze of the summer night
Why didn't you see it?

夜驾

我坐在你黑色的车里
看着你夜间驾驶
你默然无语

多伦多夜间灯火璀璨
就像银河系
我们穿梭在星际

凝视你夜间驾驶
我悄无声息
感觉又和你
在同一飞船上航行

然而
强烈的光束突然射过来
刺伤了我的眼睛
你依然无语

多年以后在我的记忆里
只有你夜间驾驶的剪影

2006.3

Night Driving

You put me into a black car
Speechless, then drove off

Like shuttling in the milk way
I saw so many bright constellations
That's Toronto at night

Sitting in that silent black car
Calmly, soundlessly
Watching you driving at night in entire silence
I felt like flying again
On board with you

But then came the light
Hurting my eyes
You didn't say anything

Now my memory
is simply a silhouette
of you driving at night

又是秋天

距离让你我之间的美变得危险
让信任变得神秘
距离摧毁了我
还有你不变的缄默
我最后的寂静

当秋天再来时
你将对我有更多的知晓
但又能怎样
很多事情将已改变
但秋天的阳光将如同从前
我脑海中的背景音乐将是另一首赞美诗

我常认为世界缺乏美
我在你身上寻找美
但我深知当我们再次相遇
你我将会改变
我们将以不同的视角
看见不同的美

秋天的开始是夏天的终结
我将不再像去年夏天那样聆听你
我的发丝将不再触及你的手臂
我的肉身将变得僵硬
对你不会再回应

是否又将是秋天
是否又将凉爽
和你在一起
就像回到家园
为什么心还想着别处
恐惧是心灵虚幻的伴侣
我们对待彼此的态度被矛盾所充满

2006.4

Autumn Again

Distance has engendered beauty between us
And encrypted trust
Distance has destroyed me
Your unchanging reticence
And my final silence

When autumn comes again
You will have known me much better
But what's the use?
So much will have changed
The light of autumn will be the same
But at the back of my mind lingered another hymn

As always, I believe the world lacks beauty
I tried to find beauty in you
But by the time we meet again
We'll definitely be different people
And we will find different beauty in different lights

Autumn begins where summer ends
But I won't listen to you as I did last summer
My hair will not touch your hand
My body will be frozen so as not to respond to you any more.

Will it be autumn again?
Will it be cool again?
My heart should feel at home when I am with you
But how come it still expects in secrecy to dwell somewhere else?
The shadow of fear keeps company of my heart, though in illusion
And ambivalent to each other we remain

梦

带着刚毅，我忍耐着——
你留下一个折磨着我的梦
火车——
越过了你的无意识和我的意识

一个关于失落和迷茫的梦，飘忽不定
火车将你带到了未知的车站
我谦卑地坐在你的身边——
我没有肉身的情人

火车上有着一群人
在我们周围
你温柔地示意我坐在你身边
于是　卑微的我成为了众人的焦点
——因为你的恩典
我却悄悄地担心着你离去时的伤悲瞬间

你并不觉知
这个梦萦绕了我整个冬季
在远方毫无猜疑地
你是否在心里
为我
涌起一丝怜惜——

关于你的这个梦中断了
不带有任何外界的声息
唯有我写下的这些静寂的诗句
将抚慰我的失落和焦虑

2005.12

Dream

With quiet fortitude I endured——
The torture of a dream you left behind
The train——
Ran beyond your unconsciousness and my consciousness

A dream of capricious loss and uncertainty
The train took you to an unknown stop
With me timidly sitting by your side——
My fleshless lover with a sacred face——

Around us on the train was a a crowd
Gently you signaled me to sit by your side
The most obscure person became the focus of attention
——Thanks to your grace
But secretly I feared the sorrowful moment of departure

Without your knowledge
The dream has been haunting me throughout the winter
Unsuspectingly in distance,
Have you ever in sympathy felt——
my loneliness amid the crowd

My dream of you came to a sudden end——
Without any external voice;
But the silence of my poems quenched my anxiety and disappointment

我建造了一艘看不见的船

我在空中录下自己的声音
我用眼睛修改自己的词句
我审查是否有任何越界——
任何个性 任何脆弱

我努力寻找礼貌的外交面纱
可以掩盖个性
否则它将过于强烈
我用裸露并且半透明的语言
越界但又无法破译

我建造了一艘看不见的飞船
一艘穿梭在生与死、宁静与痛苦之间的飞船

我乘坐这艘人们看不见的飞船
在非现实之中旅行
痛苦坐在我的左边
他深深地亲吻我
让我幻想无尽——
释然坐在我的右边
他温柔地拥抱我
带着绝望

我的飞船日夜穿行
直到在一个夜晚
遇见你

2006.2

I Built an Invisible Spaceship

I recorded my voice in the air
I reviewed my sentences with my eyes
Watching for any transgression——
Personality—— or weakness

I strived for a veil of courtesy
To cover a personality so intense
I used a language naked and opaque
Transgressive yet indecipherable

I built an invisible Spaceship
A Spaceship that shuttles between——
Life and death, tranquility and agony

I took the invisible spaceship
I travel to unreality which doesn't exist
Agony in my left
Kisses me in deeply
Evocation on my right
Hugs me gently
With a tinge of desperation

My spaceship travels day and night
Till you ask me to stop one night

在海的那一边

在海的那一边
在人口密集、高楼鳞次栉比的城市
你在地铁的人流中
走在回家的路

为什么我总是想起你
以最凄惨的悲切——
以你视为苍白的悲切
我隐士的幽居
一半被白雪覆盖

当白雪洒满灌木与深深的草丛
在海与风的距离中
让我用颤音为你唱一首歌

2005.12

On the Other Side of the Ocean

On the other side of the ocean
In a densely populated city with skyscrapers
You are one of them
Emerging from the subway
Homeward returning

Why do I always think of you?
With the voice of the uttermost woe——
With a woe that is macabre to you——
In my hermit's recesses——
Half buried by snow

我曾经拥有一个诵读者

我的诵读者比我年长无数个季节
我无法忘记他的森林和跳跃的马儿
我曾和他一起打猎
我双目紧闭
因为太羞涩

我时常后悔
当他漫步在我的丛林中时
我因羞怯而闭上双目
虽然我想看见他阳光中的面容

这是我们唯一的狩猎
我却不知道他的脸庞如何发出光芒
因为羞涩 我闭上了双目

在我的丛林中
他为我诵读故事
我睁开双眼
在昏暗中注视他的侧影
凝望他如何牵动嘴角微笑
如何闭上他的眼睛

I once Had a Reader

I once had a reader
My reader was older than me by many seasons
I can't forget his forest and his galloping horse
I went hunting with him
With my eyes closed
Because I was shy and humble

I always regret closing my eyes out of timidity
When he roamed in my jungle
Though I had wanted to see his face in the light

That is our only hunting
I don't know how his face glowed when we hunted
Because I closed my eyes
I was too shy

When could I go into his forest and touch his horse
His has a different season of life from mine
With someone else he has bought a house
And I have bought mine

打猎之后他感觉疲惫
但是他为我朗读他脑海中的书
用从不间断的温柔细语
他深深地爱着我
但他拒绝承认
因为谦卑和羞怯

我曾经拥有一个诵读者
我那时应该睁开眼睛

2009.6

My reader read me stories in my jungle
I opened my eyes
Watching his silhouette in the dim light
Watching smile creeping into the corner of his mouth
With his eyes closed
Exhausted as he was upon hunting
He read me books in his mind
In a never pausing soft whisper
He loved me deeply
But he didn't admit his love for me
because he was humble and shy

I once had a reader
I should have opened my eyes

左岸酒店

在巴黎寒冷的街道上
你是否会想起我?
或者,你已经离去——
在左岸酒店附近
一家客栈,一条街,如此繁忙
在北京的一家星巴克咖啡店
一个南瓜饼点心之后
我离开了你
我们说再见

我问一个穿着制服的侍卫:南方在哪里?
我的家在南方
我寻找着出租车
我亲吻了你的脸颊
你又变成了陌生人

不是那么绝望,而是带着希望
因为我想可能还将再次见到你
我没有犹豫,也没有哭泣
还有一夜
我并不知道
你会和我拉开距离

FX Hotel

On the cold street of Paris, have you ever thought of me?
Or you have left——
Near FX hotel, an Inn, a street, so busy
After eating a pumpkin pie at a Starbucks cafe in Beijing
We departed from each other

I asked a guard in uniform, where the south was
I lived in the south
I looked for a taxi
And I kissed you on your cheek
You became a stranger to me again

Not so despairing, but with hope
Because I thought I might see you again
I neither hesitated nor wept
There was one more night
I didn't know
You would keep me off

那一天你离去
我拨打一个后来被彻底抹去的号码
铃声响了又响
我知道你已经抵达空港
我知道你正在登机
我知道你正在疾书
铃声响了又响

我在悲伤和绝望的袭击中挣扎
直到你蓝色的文字在午夜抵达
你告诉我公路两旁的大树金黄
你说一切像个梦
你并无真正的忧虑

你喜欢潮湿的记忆
但是吹一口气就足够

关于你的过去和未来
你和她们的冒险
我不会为之困扰
左岸酒店是一刹那的共识
我们一刹那的承担

你在左岸身披的长袍
我希望再次将我的围巾遗忘

那天早晨她离开
7 点钟以前
他为她披上第二块红色的披肩
他们道别
然后他关上了门

2008.11

The day you left
I rang you at a number which I later erased for good
It rang and rang
I knew you were at the airport
You were boarding
You were writing
It rang rang rang

I lived in strokes of sadness and despair
Till your blue letter arrived at midnight
Telling me the trees along the highway were golden
It was like a dream to you
You were without real worries

You like damp memories
But a whiff must be enough

As to your past and future
You adventures with other women
I can't afford to bother
We just have one moment together
We are committed to——for just one moment——

The lovely robe you wore at FX hotel——
I hoped I could have left another scarf on the couch

That morning she left
Before 7 o'clock
But he put the second red scarf on for her before sending her off
And closed the door

我在地铁里如是想

我穿梭在黑暗隧道里
想着离太阳最近的部落
想着蓝天、白云、你

我的语言
你都不懂
你的语言对我 像天上的云

语言的缺失是迷雾
语言的缺失能止痛

失语的感觉流淌在我心口
无法流向你
穿梭在黑暗的隧道里
我想着离太阳最近的部落
我想着蓝天 白云

2015.1

I Shuttled in the Dark Tunnel

I shuttled in the dark tunnel
Thinking of the monastery which is closest to the sun
Thinking of blue sky and White Cloud

My language
You don't understand
Your language, to me, is like the white cloud in the sky

The lack of language is mist
The lack of language kills pain

The feel of Aphasia flows in my heart
But can't flow to you
Shuttling in the dark tunnel
I think of the Monastery which is closest to the sun
I think of blue sky and white cloud

馈赠

你给我的礼物
是富有革命意义的孤独

暮色中
我寻找记忆中
开满粉白花蕾的
那一颗不高的树
它依然在等着我
但粉色的花已成昨日的梦
树已经是夏天的葱绿
尽管这是四月的夜晚

花朵绽放的时间很短
就像我和你昨日的记忆
已经成为季节不复存在的残痕

夜色中
我闻到一种气息
它深深地吸引了我
那是紫色的槐花
长在很高的树上
我抬头仰望夜空中它的花簇

在那远方
你是否知道我在树下想你
你的沉默
赋予我巨大的虚空
是我冥想的空间
是我富有革命意义的孤独
尽管我的孤独浸淫着辛酸

这一份关于你的残缺的记忆
在我孤独的冥想中延伸
伸向远方的你
这就是你馈赠我的
最高的礼物

2016.4

Endowment

The gift you gave me is Solitude
Dyed in the color of revolution

One night in dusk
I looked for
The tree of pink blossoms
It was not tall
And was still waiting for me
Yet those pink flowers were already yesterday's dream
The tree was now in summer's rich green
Though it was still April

The buds sprouted evanescently
Like our memories of yesterday
Were already seasonal debris no longer existing

In darkness,
I was deeply attracted
To the strong perfume in the air
It was the purple flower
Of the tall pagoda tree
I looked up to look for its cluster

Did you knew
I was thinking of you afar under a tree?
You silence
Bestowed me with an immense void
The cosmos of my imagination and meditation
This is my solitude dyed in the color of revolution
And saturated in lonesomeness

My memory about you was incomplete and impaired
It stretched to you in the distance
This is the ultimate gift you gave me

第一次听见你说话

第一次听见你说话
我的心就开始燃烧
没有别的任何美酒
能更让人醉

我想在白色圣诞节时
飞到雪域高原来看你
可是您降临了
就像从雪域高原飘下来的一片雪花
没有肉身的恋人握住彼此的手

激情在燃烧
你怀疑我心中的火焰是为你还是为你的信仰
于是你试图将它扑灭

冲突开始了
它的阴影很长
精神恋人们永远分离了——

2015.2

First time I heard You Speak

First time I heard you speak
Exhilaration was within me
There could be no outer wine
So intoxicating

I yearned to fly to the land of snow
To see you on White Christmas
But you descended like a flake
Fleshless lovers shook hands

Passion was burning
You doubted my burning heart was for you or for your faith
And you tried to put it out

The conflict started
Its shadow was long——
Fleshless lovers would forever part——

圣殿饮茶

在你面前
我该说什么呢
不能说出心中的爱
也不能说出心中的怨

只有静默
看你凝视远方

在圣殿翅膀下你的院落里
我们只有静默
你眺望窗外
我低头
在泪光中
在你的侧影里

后来我才知道
每一个夜晚
我在远方夜空中的哭泣
可能已经让你的身体改变

可是
当我们相见
除了"你好""再见"
没有别的话语
尽管
你知道我心中所有的希望和绝望

很多年以后
我仍然会想起
那一天
在圣殿的翅膀下
我和你隔着低矮的茶桌在一起
我在泪光中凝望你的侧影
我们没有任何语言

2016.3

Drinking Tea at a Holy Monastery

What should I say when I was with you?
Neither my secret love
Nor the bitterness

In silence
I looked at your gaze into the distance

Under the wings of the holy monastery
We remained silent
You looked out of the window
I lowered my head
In tears
And in your silhouette

Later I knew
That my sob at every night far away
Had changed your body

But when we met
Except greetings
There were no other words
Though you were aware of my hope and melancholia

Many years later
I would still remember
Beneath the wings of the Holy Temple
How we sat at the tea table
When I peered at your silhouette in the twinkling tears
With no word spoken

我对你生起的心

我对你生起的心
是爱?是不爱?
我说
不是爱,也不是不爱
我对你生起的情
是恨?是不恨?

我说
不是恨,也不是不恨

不可说,不可取
说是爱,其实不是爱,只是叫作爱
说是恨,其实不是恨,只是叫作恨

我说
我终于学会了
我在想起中忘记你
我在忘记中想起你

想,不想;不是想,也不是不想
忘,不忘;不是忘,也不是不忘
想与不想
忘与不忘
皆为虚妄

爱与不爱
恨与不恨
已不复存在

2015.5

The Heart for You that I Give Rise to

The heart for you that I give rise to
Is love? Or no love?
I say

It is neither love nor non-love
The feelings for you that I give rise to
Is hate? Or no hate?
I say
It is neither hate, nor non-hate

Can't be spoken, can't be cherished
Love is not love
Therefore it is just called Love
Hate is not hate
therefore it is just called hate

I say
I have finally learned
To forget you while remembering you
To remember you while forgetting you

Think, do not think
Neither think, nor not think
Forget, do not forget
Neither forget, nor not forget

Love and not to love
Hate and not to hate
They all don't exist
And have never existed

蓝天 白雪 红袍

从印度学习十多年回来的格西
带着藏地的小阿克们在雪地里散步
他是他们的经师

十二岁的小阿克
酷酷地戴着格西的墨镜
格西的脸上洋溢着微笑
像父亲一样
爱、宁静、幸福在他的眼睛中流淌

在帝都的雾霾中
我有着很多痛苦和烦恼
但看着你们的蓝天 白雪 红袍
还有脸上的笑
我郁结的心释然了

谢谢您
土生格西和小阿克们

2015.12

Azure Sky, White Snow, and Red Kasaya

Azure sky, white snow, and red kasaya
The Gheshy who had studied 13 years in India
Was taking a stroll in the snow with the child monks
He was their sutra master

The twelve-year-old monk
Was wearying Gheshy's sunglasses so coolly
Gheshy's face was beaming
With Beaming with a fatherly smile
Love, tranquility and Happiness
were suffusing in his eyes
With his eyes exuding love, peace and happiness

In the smog of the capital's deep winter
I had so many anxieties and pains
But looking at your
Azure sky, pure white snow, red kasaya,
And the smile on your face
My melancholia dissolved

My anxieties, which were sharpened by the smog,
Dissolve in the azure sky

Thank you
Tusheng Gheshy and the child monks

下篇

致六祖

我穿越了 1300 个光年来看您
踏着青葱的绿草
跨过层峦叠嶂
一路粉桃如云

您的皮肤已经黝黑
双目低垂
进入深深的禅定
宛如 1300 年前

那一个月黑风高的夜晚
为逃避同门追杀
您辗转流徙于山岭
妒忌、背叛、阴谋
在历史的每一个时空都存在
这难道是不灭的人性?
可是您说
"菩提本无树,
明镜亦非台。
本来无一物,
何处惹尘埃。"
"不是风动,
不是幡动,
仁者心动。"

千年之后
这里依然山连着山　树连着树
行走在你曾坐禅的山中
雨后的薄暮之光
在我脸上洒落

您驻锡岭南此山中讲法三十载
为躲避权力和盛名的漩涡
你拒绝了历史长河中
东方唯一女皇的召见
她拜接你穿过的袈裟
长跪于长安城墙外

您知道
我会穿越 1300 个光年
在春雨初歇后的光晕中来看您
您皮肤黝黑　神情依然
泪水如春雨般洒落心头
我向您深深膜拜

有人设置了一道门槛
要我在购买了循环的鲜花后
才能离您更近
但是我已经相信大道至简

已经抛弃所有的钱财
跪在禅定中您的面前
在意念中我为您献上山中所有的鲜花

发阿耨多罗三藐三菩提心的善女子
令人惊讶的朴素简单
穿越无数光年
在您的神殿里
跪在沉入永恒禅定的你面前
这里是最简约的神殿

春雨初停的清澈阳光中
那个月高风清的追杀之夜又闪现
但禅定中的你抚平了一切

我穿越时空来跪拜
可是我来与不来
你都一样地空寂安然

2017.4

踏着厚厚的积雪,我来五台山看您

踏着厚厚的积雪
我来五台山看您
文殊师利菩萨千里迎接我

夜色中的五台山
白雪皑皑
千万盏智慧之灯已点亮

您的一生
被四个梦牵引
然而您说
痴愚之人才执着于梦

您不畏时间的沧桑与人间的摧残
三十年的囚禁
您说只是闭关

您说
老就是苦啊
可是在衰老的痛苦中
您还潜入我的梦境
赐予我力量和加被

您说
业不自主
我们做不了主
您嘱咐我：
必须勇猛精进
要感召暗中神圣的加持

您指点我：
读经要少而精，精而行
心要与经丝丝入扣
心就会转变

您说
菩提是从烦恼中来
您向我破解了终极咒语的秘意
您要我像莲花一样洁白地独出于污泥

您说
一切都有因果
一切都很公平
一切都是自作自受

您说
执着是妄想
不执着是圣境
可是
我还是执着地
踏着厚厚的积雪
来五台山看您
您安详地侧卧长眠
在色泽如琉璃的智慧之火熄灭之后
我看见您化为一片绚丽的舍利

在翻飞的白雪中
离别五台山
文殊师利菩萨送我八百里

2017.11

白塔山下

白塔山下
别离时
你要我在你走后
独自登上湖心的白塔山
膜拜顶礼
沙尘暴之后
天空很蓝
仿佛就在雪域

你叮嘱我：
老去之后
不要像他们一样垂钓江河湖泊
你说，应该放走所有的鱼儿
你说，我已经有了信仰
你让我每天修行不断
你说：
我老了将姿态如烟
不会惧怕死亡
死去之时将静美如秋日落叶

在这里
人们不会转经转塔
那一年

桃树枝冒出粉色花蕾的三月
你带我登上湖心小岛的山顶
和我一起转塔转经
那一天
天空没有颜色

今天，五月的一个明媚春日
天空很蓝
你让我独自涉渡登高

每一次奔向白塔
都不是孤独之旅
因为有你在那里等我
在山下的湖畔
你教我念诵咒语
因为你知道夜晚降临 我会眼泪来袭

我担心离散
你说忧虑之时分离就已经发生
你让我学会了宇宙的元音和最有加持
力的语言
你让我现在就去经受没有你的空寂

登上白塔之巅
我在像前膜拜顶礼

山巅伫立 眺望雪域
经历昨日有你时的一切

这是五月的下午
天很蓝 云很轻
空中没有飘飞的杨絮柳絮
阳光清澈透明
仿佛在雪域
你永远在等我
尽管我总是独自来去
我看见自己奔赴你
奔赴极乐、孤独的朝圣之旅

2017.5

日记，暴雨

我在夏日靠近离别的暴雨中昏睡
醒来　然后奔赴你

躲雨在地下通道，你等着我
衣衫简朴褴褛
像是一位来自月亮的流浪汉
而我知道　你是至高的行者

书店的咖啡馆已经不存在
我们在路边避雨
我说："我们就要别离——"
我的眼泪夺眶而出

可是，你用一只毛笔
开始在宣纸上书写金色的咒语
那是你馈赠给我的礼物

那年夏天我认识你时，你很淡然
今年夏天别离时，你仿佛进入禅定

你拿出一颗圣湖之心的绿松石
将它布施给街头托钵而行的乞讨者
在你行布施时

我忘记了自己动荡起伏的心境
那已夺眶而出的眼泪停止了流淌
我都还来不及哭泣
我们就要别离

穿着一双洁白的球鞋
我在暴雨中奔赴你
在雨丝中和你说再见
独自行走在浸满雨水的街头
白球鞋鞋底脱落破裂
我的双脚与地面肌肤相亲
只有你的慧眼和法眼
在雨雾中伴我砥砺前行

这个夏季没有风
这个夏季有一场暴雨

2017.7

重回布达拉

在冬日下午的斜阳里
我眺望南方的海

在海边
你红色、黄色的衣衫在飘扬
抚动着礁石、浪花
凝望着北方
你像孩子一样地微笑

拉萨下起了第一场雪
我应该紧随你磕长头在布达拉宫前膜拜
在八廓街转经

你已经游遍所有的地方
你总是说
如果时间变了
如果地点不一样
如果不是在布达拉的翅膀下
如果不是在圣城神秘的暮色中
如果不是隔着藏家庭院的天井和窗棂
将不会有凝视和相望

你是隐身的
你是被囚禁的
你说你不需要自由

每一个晚上
你总会没有踪影地在深夜等我
有人在黑暗中哭泣
有人感觉到振动的气息
有人聆听哭泣
有人为她焚香

过去你的眼神落寞有悲伤
后来你像孩子般微笑

冬日斜阳里的流泪 冥想
这里的第一场雪遥遥无望
你在海岛的浪花里赤足 眺望北方

我们想着拉萨飘落的第一场雪
我们想着何日能重回布达拉

2014.1

我不认识你

在没有光、没有电的夜晚,你会想起我吗?
打动我的音乐是否也会打动你?
让你看到我的诗句,我心里有很多恐惧
如何唤起你关于前世的记忆?
思索一直会飘落于这个问题的节点:
为什么我觉得我过去见过你?
当你那里只有黑暗和寒冷,你不告诉我
当草原的野花盛开,你也不告诉我
你说过:"我们生活在两个世界,
告诉你,你不懂,也不屑。"

总是想说:"你的这一生,是一个殉道者——"
总是想问:"你的这一生,尤其是在见到我后,是否觉得孤寂?"

我写给你的字,需要多长的刹那才能触摸到你?

年轻时的你
是如何越过冰山雪峰
抵达山的南麓
那鲜花盛开的地方?
二十多年后的你
又为何选择归来?

我如何望眼欲穿地期盼你
但我最终告诉世界我不认识你
我最终也将告诉你我不认识你

黑白琴键敲击出的音符
最终将化为洁白、透明、虚无的莲花
盛开在日轮、月轮的光晕之中
然后消失

2017.6

想起你

一阵阵悸痛
想起你
在橘黄和白色的雾霭里
在蓝色的湖光中
在没有门牌的寺院里
在河水逆向流淌的地方
在玉石温软的树林里
在雪域 在北极
在娇小精致的一簇簇红棉花下
在我出生的地方
在我所有浪迹之地
在江河的源头
在汇入大海的入口
在枫叶杂染的国度

想起你
永久的分离
永久的破裂
一阵阵沉默

梦见过你写给我的字
在心里我一直对你诉说
但在尘世中
我已经没有声音

有谁会在意
听不见的音调?

想起你
直到已经记不起你的样子
默念你
直到存在变为无相、无声、无色
无香、无触、无味,
想起你直到没有再想起你

在夏天的绚烂和湿润中
我还在想翻飞的白雪
想起你
直到光年跌倒在伤口的沟槽里
直到诗歌失去生命
音乐不再激发心灵

想起你
直到征服了不可征服的你
直到拒绝了众人膜拜和臣服的你
想起你
直到不再想起你
但也非忘记你

2017.4

我跨越了无量的海拔与您相遇

我跨越了无量的海拔与您相遇
我历经了无尽的崎岖与您相聚

然而我知道
您身披禁色
我对您的爱
不能住于相
不能住于色
不能住于身
只能住于心

您说
我的心就像藏地多变的天
您说
我刹那间就会失去自己

在无常中
我寻找恒常
在无情中
我寻找慈悲

您聆听我的哭泣
您聆听我的低语

隔着无量的海拔
隔着四季的距离

让我在清晨
无尽无量无边的梵音中
观想您
让我对您的爱
不垢不净不增不减不生不灭

2017.5

曾经

以为你在那片荆棘林后面等我
当我近乎赤裸站在你面前时
划破的衣衫和刺伤的身体
将是我为爱而跋涉的见证

在无尽的黑暗中
在无边的荆棘里
我穿行
与痛楚和黑暗搏击
对你的向往
让我披荆斩棘
在皎洁的月光下
我终于到达树林的尽头

曾经
我在浓香弥漫的春夜冥想你
曾经
我突破心灵的瓦砾默念你
曾经
你是我内心神秘的花园
曾经
我以为只有你才能破解我快乐的密码

对你的向往
原来只是我的执念

在荆棘林的尽头
披荆斩棘后的我
赤裸站立 鲜血淋漓
可是你已经消失
化为了那片我已穿越的黑暗荆棘林

在月光下
我已无所顾盼
心不再禁锢于往昔的痛苦和执迷
只专注于当下如银的月光
在这个春日的夜晚
我已经
越过荆棘
越过你
我已经
明心见性

2017.4

灵光古刹

莫名的疲惫与绝望
又袭击了我

西藏小女孩
将要来陪伴我
和我一起去灵光寺
膜拜佛牙舍利塔

灵光寺
佛牙舍利塔
多年来一直呼唤我前往
可我突然又深陷囹圄
在流沙中陷落又挣扎

我问我的另一个西藏孩子
扎多学长,
他来自和不丹毗邻的亚东
"我的藏文小老师,
佛牙舍利究竟有何殊胜?"

小小扎多说:
"佛牙的保护令人惊羡,
其实佛牙舍利本身没什么神奇,

但不知道为什么,
在舍利面前,
就从内心深处升起一种说不出的感受,
或许这就是信仰——"

不知为什么
近日流沙又突然来袭
我该如何在绝望中忆念
拉萨大昭寺里
那满月般皎洁的脸庞
拉卜楞寺
老上师智慧慈悲关爱的眼光

当他们都在追逐世间目标
我的西藏小女孩
就要来看我
将陪我度过黑夜
扎多学长叮嘱说
我们天不亮就要早起
去灵光寺膜拜的人会很多

白塔山下
师父早已经告诉我们
膜拜灵光寺佛牙舍利和大昭寺的等身佛像
得到的加持一样

朝圣佛牙舍利塔
只因心灵的感应
那是很久以前就种下的愿望
虽然疲惫和绝望又来袭
可是突然有天使般的西藏小女孩
引领陪帮我
我们将一起朝圣佛牙舍利塔

2017.6

五台山

白色茫茫中
驶向文殊北台的山路上
我看见他们
从渐起的迷雾中合十走来

五台山上寺庙无数
他们虔诚的脚步停留于每一个膜拜之处
哪怕那个寺庙看上去破败衰落

迷雾
在山际的草原上升起
逐渐浓厚

我们坐在车中
看这群徒步的朝拜者
穿越山际草地一片又一片
而雨和雾时弱时猛

车
在白色雨雾中
驶向无垢文殊北台
雾气缭绕
但刹那间

雾气又飘散
我们盘桓在逶迤的山路

在不可穿透的白雾中
我们行驶
聆听雨滴敲打车顶
羊群在窗外吃草
偶尔会抬头凝视我
在不远处
一群群白色或杂色的羊群在漫步

浓雾消散后又升起
雨声更紧凑
青石板路就像群山的腰带
我们举步维艰
心也在迷雾中颠簸
但路旁吃草的奶牛还是不紧不慢
焦虑无法突破迷雾

向东行
向东行
迷雾散尽
雨声渐停
无垢文殊北台青白色的庙顶
在白色的雾气中显现

简约、庄严

清白色石砌的寺庙里
金铜色的佛像前
我长跪
祈求能获得无垢的智慧
和我一起跪下的
是一位纯洁虔诚的少女

多年以后回望才知晓
无垢文殊菩萨就在那时
给予了我们终身的加持和庇佑

2015年8月朝拜五台山
2016年7月15日凌晨
整理于拉萨邦达仓

各莫之旅

前世，雪域的一对姐妹
今生，在末法时代迷失

那时
生下来就有信仰
那时
家园离天堂很近

这一生，沉沦在浊世
关于信仰的记忆，只有慢慢苏醒

妹妹投生在金沙江头
姐姐投生在扬子江尾
这是同样的一条
由雪山之水汇聚而成的母亲河
在雪域，它的名字叫雅鲁藏布江
在汉地，它的名字叫金沙江，长江，或扬子江

关于雪域和信仰的记忆
逐渐苏醒
姐姐站在尼泊尔的发愿塔
许下心愿：
这一生一定要升起菩提心

妹妹望穿了四季
奔赴草原
奔赴这一世最伟大的老上师
奔赴菩提心法会

各莫，草原上神圣的寺院，就在眼前
闪烁着佛舍利的金光
妹妹看见正在被定格的姐姐
手中托起了金塔
姐妹今生第一次相遇

妹妹说：
她前世的家乡就在雪域
她的虔诚、勇敢
还有胸前那串圣洁的念珠
让姐姐觉得似曾相识

白云奔涌在蓝天
像一群骏马
金色的寺庙前
老上师的法语梵音中
妹妹泪流满面
天空中飘扬着一条条洁白的哈达
姐姐说：她的前世是雪域的牧民

一切法无我
得成于忍
关于前世的记忆
在今生忍辱中苏醒

但不可纠缠于前世与今生
因为今生就是来生的前世

飘散在三千大千世界碎为微尘的姐妹
在开满鲜花的草原相遇又散去

为了来世
珍惜今生

菩提心
随着太阳
每一天都在姐妹俩的心中升起

2017.8

在雪域

在雪域
没有肖邦的钢琴、致郁的音乐
只有转经的念诵、磕长头的咒语

在雪域
他们将永远不会和你对视
为了清净的戒律

在雪域
你的头上打开了一把高高的白伞盖
为你消除情仇 扭转逆缘障碍

在雪域
恶狼对你狂吠
你对他说：谢谢
在雪域
野猪在你磕长头时
衔走了你的念珠

在雪域
夜空深蓝
星空下的院子是他的家
你驻足凝望

然而你知道
必须消除自己的好奇
成就他的圆满清静

在雪域
夜晚一直下雨　天空常常阴霾
直到你遇见云姐姐
她美丽、她智慧
是一位令人生畏的性感愤怒女
她的才华无人能及
她的身世坎坷流离

一切还没有太迟
在雪域

2017.9

给小阿克

虔诚的母亲
将她最爱的儿子
献给佛
她创造生命
是为了供养佛
延续僧

最聪慧最优秀的男孩
在晒经滩的院落里长大
他写下一首首诗
就像地里长出一株草
树枝萌发一片叶
原本,他可以成为最伟大的诗人

母亲的爱和信仰
将他终身定格
他毫不迟疑地将自己的诗篇碎为纸屑
仿佛拔去一株草,抖落一片叶
他将只留下对佛的赞美诗

他屏息制作多玛
他入定持咒念经
他凝神击鼓 手持法器

在清水的晒经滩
他的院落
树木从枯到荣 从荣到枯
窗外的山
从青翠葱茏 然后 白雪皑皑

在冥想中
他构建出最美丽的坛城
描绘出唐卡色彩华丽
所有的参数
都和经书吻合

然而他放弃了关于画布和画笔的梦想

在拜佛的日子里
他的鼓声和梵音
感动了所有朝圣的母亲
她们都潸然泪下
在他的面前长跪

他实现了很多母亲的愿望

2017.10

定格

感谢这一瞬间的定格
让我永远留在了您的身边
和您一起守望群山

为了配搭您红色的光晕
我穿上了来自尼泊尔的白衬衫

守护在您的身边
我是快乐的天使
我是勇敢的卫士

我们一起守望群山
窗玻璃里折射着绵绵山峦

您的家就是诗歌的殿堂
我曾在那里听您讲授经典

您的家
是世间最简洁、最神圣的庭院

守候在您的身边
我像天使一样快乐
我像卫士一样勇敢

2018.7

你零点来信

四季皆有沼泽在等候
我陷入了结冰的那一个

你零点来信
让我不要围困在自己的冰窟窿里
要我关注飞鸟 游鱼 蚂蚁 昆虫

你说
如果我能关注他们的挣扎和悲哀
我必将忘却自己的挣扎和悲哀

夏天在雪域时
我是那样精进
出门前
要念诵足咒
上课前
要念诵字母咒
回到我的世界
无量的业惑又将我捆缚

你说
对自我的过度关注与珍爱
必将导致身心的崩溃

你要我去远方
或者观想远方
关注远方动物的悲欢离合

爱不能太有中心
否则爱会太裸露,太单薄

该如何在爱的同时冲破爱?
该如何接受命运的同时建造命运?
在你的注视下
我在四季中穿梭
求索答案

2018.5

猫的独白

这个世界
好人层出不穷
坏人也层出不穷

我愿意做一只
守护主人
躲在树后面暗中观察的猫

我愿意
生活在主人的家里
在他窗前的野花里散步
聆听梵音
当他看书时
我轻捷地越过窗棂
悄无声息地匍匐在他身边
听他翻阅经书的沙沙声
看他冥想凝神

在人道
辛劳至死
那些自以为拥有自由的人
其实并不自由

主人很温柔
我也很温柔
主人的生活很简朴
我的生活也很简朴

有钱人的宠物
往往肥得走不动
但我永远轻捷

我的主人
智慧广博如大海
慈悲沉默如大地
我的主人
菩提心 修梵行

比起你们
我的一生很短
但很恬淡
我每天陪伴主人诵经念咒
有时躲在树后观察进出这个院子的人

我的一生
和主人在一起
平静又祥和
我不需要去远方

主人的诵经声已经为我昭示了远方
我不需要自由
主人给了我最大的自由
我甚至超越了生死的痛苦
因为主人深知生死的奥义
如果有一天我死去
他将超度我的亡灵

如果我转世
我还愿意投生为主人家的一只猫
当有客人来时
我躲在树后暗中观察
客人走后
我在窗棂上聆听主人念咒
在他翻阅经书时
我跳进去　在他身边趴下
陪伴他念经
畜生道的我
很幸福　很宁静

2017.12

那时的我

这世界充满着太多的苦难
对你的想念
一不小心
就变成一种执念
所以
你必须沉默如大地
所以
你必须广阔如大海

让我深深地忏悔吧
这世界需要不断地忏悔
一切没有太明显的界限
信仰和眷恋
想念和执念

我时常遭受焦虑的痛苦
这一颗心
如何才能平静舒缓

我不愿意像那蚊蝇
在你的院落悲哀地合唱
升起又沉落

让我像那条河

带着某种使命
为了滋润,为了净化
流过你居住的地方
悄无声息

让我像想念远方一样地想念你
就像 12 岁时的我
——长江边的那个眺望远山的小姑娘

修行在
城市的车流和乌鸦的叫声中
我有着朝圣者的灵魂
但迷惘和抑郁的流沙会袭击我
我有时
郁郁寡欢　依榻而卧

我想念家乡 想念你
忏悔对你的想念
担心想念会变成执念
会玷污美好

让我又回到少女时代
那时我经常眺望远方
那时我纯洁又坚强
那时我心中已有爱

2017.11

秋日雨夜

寒流来袭
秋日的雨夜
如果疲惫
就安然入眠吧
如果深夜醒来
就坦然地翻阅一首诗
思索诗行后面的海洋和桅杆

或念经　或持咒
不必挣扎着再入睡

寒冬就在前面
他将归来
他将离去
爱会相续
爱又裂断

生活在故乡以北的雾霾之都
很少有秋雨用一整天
滴落成夜晚

早早地入眠
早早地在黑暗中醒来

想着雨雾的黄昏中
那一朵深秋的玫瑰
正在绽开
红色中浸透着
高贵的、凋零的黄色

我这里正下着秋雨
你那里已经飘着冬雪
你隔着窗户背靠群山
火炉里的木炭正燃烧着
当你对他们讲述生死奥义时
希望你会　想起我

2017.10

致俗女

不管你多么美丽,多么有才华
来到拉卜楞
你将只是一名俗女
即使你愿意为阿克们擦靴子
他们都不要

就算你有很多金钱
来到拉卜楞
你的钱财将只是粪土
你自以为是地开着一辆豪车
你的飞扬跋扈
只是那里人们心中的笑料

如果你是一名虔诚的俗女
就在那里心无杂念地膜拜
不要让贪嗔痴又支配了你
不要企图在那里买房
那里不是你的地方
你只是一片枯败的黄叶
飘到了那里
圣地属于圣人
黄叶不要飘落到红色的肩头
不要让大师将你弹落尘土

尽管你向往香巴拉
如果你的心不够清静
请不要披上你不配的颜色
因为那高贵的颜色
会让你显现原形
而你的原形会让很多人失望

在草原的骤雨里
你的污垢被洗掉
在草原的彩虹下
你向往香巴拉
回到城市的泥潭中
你一直挣扎着要再次奔向圣地

可是
拉卜楞不是你的家
虔诚的俗女
你只是飘过白色僧舍前的一片黄叶

不要让执念控制你
不要有奢望

让圣地归于圣人
在膜拜之后
俗女
请回到你的家乡

2017.11

奔向拉卜楞

小白马
和我一起去拉卜楞吧
那里有你前世的记忆

和我一起拜见我的老喇嘛
和我一起去我的老师格西家

所有的西藏孩子中
只有你记得你前世的寺院

拉卜楞其实没有我浪漫的情怀
那里只有我虔诚而现实的思考

第一次来到拉卜楞时
我想念西藏的美丽
第一次离开拉卜楞时
我不知道为何流下眼泪
不明白为什么那里有很多红衣人

因为想念老喇嘛
我多次奔向拉卜楞
因为何种的因缘啊
我来到格西家

听他讲经说法
信心因此在我心中升起
我确信格西知道生死的奥妙

来自西藏的孩子们
已经不再憧憬神圣的使命
唯有你 小白马
清楚地记得你的前世
唯有你，小白马
还记得那一份向往
唯有你小白马
曾经想当小喇嘛

拉卜楞没有夏天
在秋天到来之前
让我带着你
我们一起去拜见老喇嘛
我们一起拜见格西
去格西家

2018.2

断灭

为了保护您的冰清玉洁
想念您,我也不能告诉您

没有您的消息
我只能忏悔我的想念是否不洁
尽管也许是因为文化的差异

您的广博
降服了我的骄傲
在您的面前
我谦卑如尘土

在没有您消息的黑暗日子里
我从不怀疑
也从不抱怨

我愿意放下一切
为了您的冰清玉洁
当想您的前念生起时
我即刻就斩断后念
念诵《金刚经》

2018.4

接受

这是上帝的安排
让我们静默如谜
让我们属于不同的语言

你属于远方
你属于白塔
你属于梦境
你的使命是让我感到力量
你的使命是让我走出抑郁的沼泽地
你来到古都
和我共同呼吸白色的雾霾
但你对我说
你在很远的地方

这是佛的安排
让我跨入您的庭院
让我听您讲经说法
让我看见你背靠群山
让我永远看见你翻阅那本古老的书

我已经谦卑如尘土
我知道你和我同时感受着古都心脏的悸动
但我无怨无悔地接受了见不到你的安排

我谦卑地接受一切
接受自己对你的想念
接受梦中对你的找寻
接受你只属于梦境的这个现实

在昨夜的焦虑和愁绪散去后
我接受了这个真理：
你属于远方和信仰
我只能在心灵之湖的深处
看到你的倒影和存在

2018.5

妮妮的独白

你们要我舞一曲
那就跳起来吧
我是真正的舞者 腰肢纤细
即使到了生命的秋季

我沉默
从不轻易在公众场合起舞
但我并不惧怕
虽然我拒绝炫耀自己的舞姿

我是一尊千面雕像
妩媚甜蜜 刚毅坚韧
齐腰的长发会被我一刹那剪断
我多变 时尚
头发的颜色会自由地在色谱中游走

我穿越时空
黄果树瀑布
上海虹口公园
中原最大的城市

我流着北方游牧民族的血液
背负着沉重的历史

见证了王朝的衰落
深深懂得贵族与平民的爱恨情仇

我懂厚重的历史
懂现实的无情
懂变迁
懂艺术和现实的距离

我懂桥牌
会择时出示
技术牌 艺术牌 文字牌
懂边缘与主流的关系

我懂很多
但是我沉默
我的骨子里是舞者 是战士

2018.3

栀子花

那个夏天的夜晚
我走在在你的窗外
风很透明
我的心也很透明

我不敢敲你的窗
当我走过你的房间时
我看见里面已经有人
坐在你的床头
我对自己说:"啊,那不是我。"

风很清凉
有着栀子花白色的清香 很浓郁
我的衣衫被鼓起
黑暗的风在我的腿间穿行
我的心好像在悬崖上跳动
不知下面有多深

我看见
你和他们一同走进了夏夜
消失在绿黑色的树丛中
透明的夜晚太黑
我找不见你的脚印

月光下栀子花灌木丛的影子
黑暗、茂密
我知道我不应该跟随你去
我知道你消失的林中有美丽的仙女

那一年夏天开始的时候
我在我的窗前种了栀子花
白色的花蕾还没开
就纷纷发黄、发黑、枯萎

那个夏天
我的心已经很疲惫
我的身体已经没有知觉
我以为我就要死去

见到你的时候
是在夏天的晨光中
空气中弥漫着白色栀子花的浓香
见到你的时候
我的脸上就有了欢笑和光芒
好像江风又吹到了我黯淡的脸上

我的目光仰望着你
我的目光追随着你

直到你和他们一起消失在夏夜的树丛
直到我的眼睛无法穿透夏夜的黑暗

那一个夏天
我的心已经很疲惫
我的身体已经没有知觉
我以为我就要死去

站在你窗前的我
觉得夏天的夜很清亮
栀子花的香味很浓烈
我总也呼吸不够
在我的腿间不断穿梭的夜晚的风
重新让我感到了黑暗的深沉

就在那个夏天的晚上
我等待着你
凝望着你
失去了你

就在是那个夏天的晚上
我的心被触摸、感动并且慌乱
就在在那个夏天晚上
我选择了生 而不是死
站在你已经离去的窗前

2006.2

地形图

我担心
如果见到你
我会突然滴下眼泪

我绘制了很多幅地形图
水的颜色是绿色的阴影
陆地的颜色是希望

你到过的城市
有的在海边 被水草湮没
有的在中原 黄沙弥漫
那是我的手指
很难扑捉的经纬

我还被覆盖在
冬天的积雪中
而你已经走过了夏天

夜晚
我在空调的噪音和凉风中
描绘着地图
你的足迹
将遍布雪山 草地 天池

我的打印机
没有颜色
我的地形图凹凸不平
画出来的水比陆地更平静

斑驳的地形图
有半岛 有沙漠 有海洋中的岛屿
有我的家乡 低洼的盆地
有历史的创伤和荣光

我陪着你
走过每一座城市
我的手指抚摸你的每一个足迹

我的地形图
血红 暗绿 透明 灰黄
地理学家从未见过的的颜色

见到你的时候
我的脑海中
会闪现出我绘制过的地形图

你的面容黯淡
你的目光犀利
却看不见我心中的地形图

如果我不小心
会滴下眼泪
然后 在都市的噪音中
我们走向地铁 说再见

2006.6

20 岁的礼物

多年前
对你的爱
让我变为了一只鸟
焦虑是我的每一片羽毛
对你的爱
让我变成了一尾鱼
所有的鳞片都折射着不安

我因此受到
诅咒与蔑视
我遭受非人的痛苦
直到
我对你的爱成为碎片
直到
所有可见的道路在我眼前都封闭

后来
我成为一株草
在那些难以理解的愤怒中
被奔跑的你所践踏
黑暗
让我恐惧 让我目眩

我从未滋生恨
总会想起你赋予我的幸福记忆

我已成为一株草
扎根于土地
当火焰逼近
鉴于心中不灭的爱
我只有求助于神秘的力量

我束缚于这颗星球上
凝视着无尽的黑暗
偶尔低语着独白
更多的时候
我忘我而且无我

对你的爱就在昨夜
然而已成为幽渺的远古
如今我只是一株被任意践踏的草
我已经没有荣辱

有一种力量
让我将焦虑变为了祈祷
让我将自己填充得强大完满
让我放下一切来祈祷
为了遏制火焰

2018.1

情人

在西贡的码头
一位 14 岁的法国少女遇见你
你 27 岁,来自中国的北方

在上海外滩
一位 18 岁的中国姑娘遭遇你
你 27 岁,来自印度南部

在波士顿
一位西藏女人认出你
你 27 岁,来自阿拉伯

深夜的警报声响起
站在你身边惊慌失措的女人
因为你的存在而觉得安全
你长得像圣战的恐怖分子
但你是唯一能带来安全感的恐怖分子

岁月已经侵蚀她
你已经认不出她
她的心已变为海参
在认出你之后
她将自己切成两半:

一半被回忆吞没
一半在现实中逃逸

在西贡和上海
她知道如何靠近你
今夜在波士顿
她只懂得分割自己
分割为心的依恋和肉体的独立
她看见
青春其实是沉重的肉身
她看见
脱离了肉体的情感 自生自灭

过去是无量劫中的相遇
是否给你留下记忆？
在波士顿的警报声中
在仓皇逃窜的人群中
你的阿拉伯眼睛告诉她：
 "I am here with you,
 You will be all right."

岁月的磨砺
已经让她变为海参
危难当头时
她自切
一半是现实一半是回忆
一半是肉体一半是诗歌
用你不懂的文字碎语

2018.2

暴雨没有降临

等待了一夜的暴雨没有降临
但起床后
我发现窗外的世界变湿润了
我的窗户所能俯瞰的花园宁静而墨绿

看那通向花园的地下车库
多少人或因需要或因富有而去购买一辆汽车
而我一直有着一份坚守
要成为一条恐龙一个古迹

在与时俱进的古都某个接近中午的早上
我没有因为晚起而责备自己
推开窗户
以牧羊人的姿态眺望远方
尽管远方只是灰色的高楼
楼下是一片睡梦之中暴雨后湿润的花园
花园的下面是地下车库

想着学生们正在艰难地应付考试
这正是他们炼狱般的考试季
但我对他们总是用心过多
感情总是大于需求
他们的一切总是结束得比我预计的早

想着如何让自己离开自己远游
如何让自己与自己的过去疏离
如何让自己与自己的现在陌生
如何回望、眺望、静观自己的一切

没有责备自己晚起
静静地沏上一壶新的菊花茶
开始我长长的、宁静而剧烈的瑜伽运动和冥想
这就是我,一条恐龙,一个化石
在积水潭附近
京都夏日某一天的开始

2017.6

归宿

路的尽头
你在那里等我

我们最后的家
石碑上刻着你我的名字
很窄小,在城市的边缘
远离喧嚣
我们将静静地在一起
把喧嚣留给尘世

我曾带着你北上南下
为了能一起走上更长的一段路
但是你还是离去
留下一个奥义
我一直挣扎着领悟:
一切如梦幻泡影
韶华音容化为一把灰烬 迅疾变迁

可是你仍然
叮嘱我走完你走过的路
你让我在沙滩上再修建一个家园和城堡
你却说
我最后的家不在沙滩上

而在路的尽头

我将带着你的期盼
去爱另外一个女人
然后,在生命的尽头
奔赴爱情最后的一场约会

你在那里等我
我们将相拥而卧
溘然长眠

2017.4

我在时光广场等你

我在时光广场等你
这里的天空常常很白
五彩的郁金香开了又谢了
莲花绽放了又消失了
人们来了又走了
只有我一直在这里
抗击着时光那淹没一切的浪潮

我在时光广场等你
眺望山河的那一边
芳草萋萋的坟头
我每天都在这里
直到白色的天空化为湛蓝

你已经是一把灰烬,无相
我已经成为一名游吟诗人
谱写死亡的安魂曲,爱情的咏叹调
我将成就今生最无量的布施

在时光广场
我踯躅 眺望
有善女子
在落英缤纷的踏青时节

为我们的故事写一首诗
然后独自匍匐在窗台落泪
有善男子
诵读我为你写的"江城子"
他的悲恸与愁绪在春天回荡

你走以后
我每一天都斋戒
像落魄孤魂在时光广场游荡
恋人的咖啡屋因为我而改变容颜
成为白昼的乌黑棺木
夜晚的水晶宫殿

亡妻
今天是你的祭日
我为你斋戒
我的已经化为一把灰烬的亡妻
你已成为我今生的信念

2017.5

照片

那一个秋日
我们爬上山巅
你说,如果再给你一次机会
你不会选择生
因为获得生命的通道太长太苦太慢
你说你不再留恋娑婆轮回
你宁可选择寂灭涅槃

那一路
我双手捧着一大把新摘的雏菊
我们从山巅下来
你所养育的生命,那个小男孩
为我定格了这一
手捧野花的黑白瞬间

我们住进
铺满鹅卵石的庭院
我赤裸着脚一次又一次地穿越
为了抵达秋千下有信号的自由地带

那时
我牵挂着两个远方的人
我刚刚走出地狱
登上证悟之旅

不顾鹅卵石抵脚的疼痛
我无数次奔向秋千下
信号能抵达的自由地带
为了远方的他们
他们互不相识
如今
一个和我的关系已经酷烈地终结
一个和我的缘分还像深山溪涧般蜿蜒

后来
你和我
仍然在帝都的雾霾中
忍辱精进地恪守一份世俗的生活
你被逃遁的渴望驱使
在海边修了一座白色的小屋

你常常说要再次带我逃离
逃离到海边

但今天
在翻阅往昔的书页时
我突然发现了这张黑白的照片

2017.2

给青江

青江
我在夏虫的鸣叫中牵挂你
想着你如何挣扎起床
哺育那嗷嗷待哺的小生命
忍受着伤口的剧痛

总是告诉自己
教学生 爱学生
就像布施河里的鱼儿
不要期盼鱼儿会回来

可是
有一条鱼儿
每年都会穿过江河
回来看我

对你说过很多次
对你的牵挂
我想穿越这座没有风的城市来看你
在你最虚弱、最坚强的时候来到你身边

想着少女时代的你
如何被我戏剧课上的故事打动

如何书写出"百合花的埋葬"
你的第一篇文学批评
想着少女时代的你
如何穿越校园对我说:
"老师,我要读研,就在你这里。"
想着我如何对你说:
"年轻姑娘本来就美,
不需要眼影。"

想着研究生时的你如何在教室门口等我
交给我本科学生的试卷和作业
你是我最恪守职责的助教

想着你
想着我后来如何逐渐地
在你身上感觉到了一份忧伤
想着我如何在你身上看到了我自己
想着我们在一起的缄默

想着我
如何忧伤而欣慰地
和你短暂相聚在每年九月的第十天
想着喜欢躲避的我总是迎接你
想着我们忧伤的沉默和力量
想着我们如何忍受了生活的伤痛

如何让爱存留

总是想着
要穿越这个无风的夏季去看你
总是想着
抱起你创造的生命奇迹
而你会在一旁欣慰地微笑
想着我一直对自己说:
要给你一份你今生缺失的爱

在明晃晃的夏日午后
想着你产后的伤痛和幸福
青江
祝福你

2017.7

最后一课

我爱了你们
不多也不少

我爱了你们
不长也不短

我爱你们
其实爱得多了一点

其实,我真的很爱你们
如果在我年轻的时候
我会因为别离而伤悲
但现在
我已经能淡然转身

你们让我再次领悟
忠诚与背叛
有情与无情
你们让我深陷信任的福地
同时遭受流沙的袭击
你们让我顿悟后渐悟
让我更加明白缘起性空

我爱你们
爱得坦荡 无私
当背叛袭击我
我也没有踉跄
反而感谢背叛

阳光灿烂
是怎样美丽的校园啊
今日何日兮?
得以和你们同舟

我不得不在最后一课
在定格的最后一瞬间
在海浪声中
用诗句将你们轻轻呼唤
希望你们以后在尘埃中
拥有一颗不失光泽的心

这样美丽的夏日
仍然有浓雾来袭

别离时
他们喜欢说些鼓满风帆的话
只有我才知道
隔着白色的雾霭

在上完最后一课
在定格最后一瞬间后
我们是怎样淡出彼此的视野

2017.6

西蜀江边盼日出

在西蜀低洼的盆地
无风的早晨
闷热潮湿的江边
我等你

想着昨日你来的时候
我是怎样满面生辉 笑容灿烂
想着你来的时候
我是如何珍惜你最温柔的一刻
想着很快
你如何变得强烈
我不得不收起我的画布、毛笔、油彩

今天我等你
站在同样的江边阳台
昨日的油画
还需要完成最后一笔

不能两次眺望同样的天空
正如不能两次踏入同样的河流
即使你来赴约
天空也不一样
云彩也不一样

你也不一样

我该如何完成昨日的油画
所需的最后一笔?

我沐浴 熏香 穿上了最美的衣裳
将母亲种的茉莉花摘下两朵
插在耳边发髻
在清香中等你

有人欺骗、背叛了我
午夜时分
心已经寂灭
今晨为了救赎 为了灭度
我又将你眺望

你没有来
可是天空还是越来越亮

在冥想中
大日如来
我祈请你的光彩

2017.8

想起苏东坡,在春风并不沉醉的夜晚

春风吹拂过夜晚
带着凉意并无醉意
过客仍在奔走
想起昨夜想起今晨
世界掠过心头又淡去
如阳光下消融的雪泥中鸿雁的印迹
一切皆如时光之河中的水珠在明灭

曾经通过一个黑暗的隧道
被挤压到这个世界
那一次
有人替她分担投生的痛苦

后来
在阳光下
她摇摆着　花枝招展
在暮日
她将萎缩成真理

世界消融时
痛苦将无人分担
她将再次经过一个通道
或遁入六道轮回
或进入极乐世界

带着这份悲伤的阵痛
过客行驶在春风拂过的无眠夜晚

2018.4

道歉

我向我绝对信任过的人道歉
你说这个世界上谁也不能绝对信任
你很快以身示法

我向旧日的恋人道歉
因为我待新来者如同初恋

我向我曾为他们写过抒情诗的人道歉
因为文字虽在
但我的窗户已经不再打开

我向家乡道歉
因为我没有留恋

我向被遗忘的爱情和亲情道歉
因为我的诗歌没能让你们免遭遗忘

我向静寂的钢琴曲道歉
因为我已经感到你们的吵闹、重复或者单调

我向心理大师们道歉
因为我以智慧和慈悲洗刷心灵的污染
其实我不想让你们丢失饭碗

我向信仰道歉
因为我善于质疑

我向阳台上的植物道歉
因为我不能在空中变出连着大地的土壤
所以我不再把你们浇灌

我向团体和机构道歉
因为我相信这本书(《乌合之众》)

我向鱼儿道歉
虽然将你放生
但仍避免不了你再次陷入渔网的宿命

我向我自己道歉
虽然我能预知很多事情
但无法改变任何轨迹

我向远方的男人道歉
虽然我不断地为你写诗
其实我并不爱你

我向至今仍然在乎我的人道歉
因为我什么都已经不在乎了

2018.5

用尽一生的时间

用尽一生的时间
明白爱常常处于灰色地带

用尽一生的时间去成长
用尽一生的时间去适应
用尽一生的时间去学会不执着

用尽一生的时间明白：
爱恨皆为障碍
爱可以和欺骗共存

用尽一生的时间去理解
爱如何变为不爱
忠诚如何变为背叛

用尽一生的时间
学会独立
用尽一生的时间
去理解因缘的聚合
用尽一生的时间
学会尊重缘分
学会随缘、不攀缘分
用尽一生的时间
学会了拥有一份尊严

用尽一生的时间
去领悟古典音乐的沉重

用尽一生的时间学会淡定
其实，不需要一生的时间
同样的灾难
第二次发生时
惊慌失措已经变为从容淡定

用尽一生的时间理解何为生老病死
用尽一生的时间
在生命最后的节点
才明白无常是生命唯一的常态

2018.5

给 Justine

Justine
你怎么会知道
我深夜独自在灯前
翻拍我们唯一的照片
它贴在你送我的那本
Thesaurus 字典的扉页

站在你熟悉的校园一角
在那一片郁金香的花海
我眺望着远方异度空间的你

越过这一片灿烂的花海
我望着你
海风拂过尘世
静静地呼啸而过
在我的耳畔
我听见你的声音
这一切是我没有想到的结局
校园里春光点点
只是没有你熟悉的飞舞柳絮

我听见
你的声音像落蝶一般寂寞

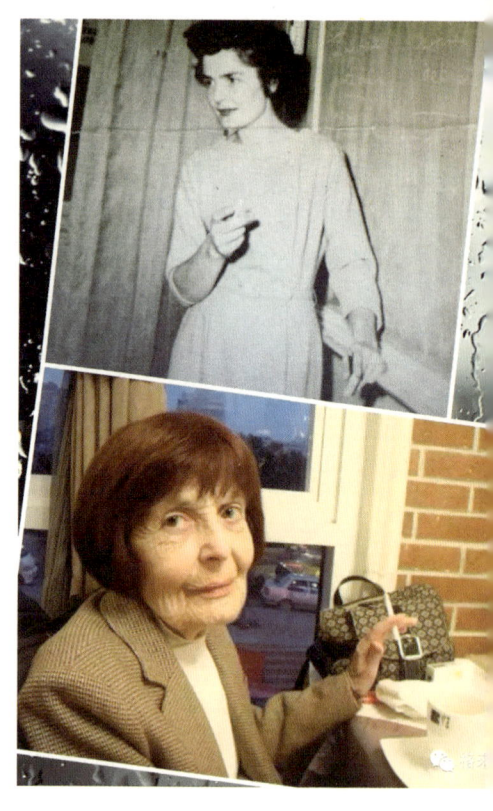

隔着海洋和陆地
隔着白天和昼夜
向我诉说你的痛苦和焦虑
以及对死亡的预感

贝壳里传来海的哭泣
是谁在聆听着谁的诉说？
你已经离去了这么久
我才明白
为什么一直没有了你落蝶般的声音

任春天的柳絮四处飘散
溢出这一片眼泪的海洋
我站在校园这片郁金香的花海畔
眺望你在波士顿的墓园
那里一定绿草如茵
春光斑斓

2016.4

给婆（1）

很多人的生活
因为一个人而成为悲剧

因为一个人的错误
在饥荒的废墟上　成片的人倒下

因为一个人的无知、自卑和固执
在饥饿和死尸的废墟上
无数的生命又开始繁殖
——最终将酿成另一个灾难

什么样的土壤
什么样的空气
导致对生命如此的践踏

因为一个人的错误
她的华年被荒废
但一个女婴因此而被她抚育

走下讲台的教师
韵华正茂，但成了保姆
大学里的学生变成了她带过的十几个婴儿
手中翻动的书页成了片片尿布

长江边
一个潮湿的城市
有一条深深的小巷
天天从那里进出的女人已经佝偻年老
她替人看过的十几个孩子都纷纷长大离开
但那个大眼睛的小姑娘总是会回来看她

她从不抱怨她的命运
她仍然热爱她的组织
她总是给小姑娘讲述同样的故事

在时间停滞的海洋中
记忆已经看不见将来
她认为回来看她的小女孩是 27 岁而不是 36 岁

小姑娘在她身边长大
小姑娘走出了长江穿过的那个盆地
那阴影却始终无法驱散

那一天终于到来了
她只能记忆起过去
而不能感知现在和将来

2005.3

给婆(2)

如果菜畦已变成街道
如果农舍已变成商场
如果孤独坚定的黑色布鞋已经变得老迈蹒跚摇晃
如果轻快跳跃的双脚已变得沉重哀伤
如果那个旁人觉得她孤独但她并不孤独的身影已经需要搀扶
如果那个雀跃的少女已经憔悴压抑怅惘
不是如果
而是已经

如果在这城市化的山顶上
老年女人的记忆已经丧失
年轻女人的方向已经消散
如果多年以后的一次散步
一老一少已经找不到回去的路
已经不知道走到了记忆的何方
不是如果
而是已经

时光是否在倒流
时光或许已经停止
时光已经不能带来悲痛
时光分离
时光相聚

记忆的失落　感情的停滞

找不到走出时光隧道的路
透明的白色隧道
空气永远那样湿润
在一个城市化的山顶上

2006.2

给贾斯汀——关于《英国病人》

是孤独在敲击着吉他的琴弦
还是吉他在敲击着孤独的心弦?

这是悲伤的礼拜堂
塔尖笼罩着云彩
教堂的剪影是在晨光中
还是在暮色里?
在英语里
这是同一个单词:dusk

我能看见
黑暗之神穿着柔软的丝质拖鞋
袭击了你
你失去了语言
但你的思维永远敏捷
你永远是果断的决策者
智慧而勇敢的女人
这一次你决定了对生死的选择
你对尘世已经没有留恋
你拒绝现代医学的起死回生术
你选择了荒芜的古代
你选择休息三天后
进入不醒的长眠

你给我的传承
已经让我成为一名歌者
我总在想
你试图摆脱沉重和萎缩的肉身时
是否遭受了太多的痛苦?
或者只是昏沉沉地坠入长眠?

我的身上
总是最容易留下痕迹
来自清教故乡的你
传承给了我清教徒对情感的压制
但我们也渴望自由和超脱

离开东方的那一天
你给我一本发黄的书
它至高的主题
是模糊疆界、杂糅身份
如果你知道
我将成为诗的女儿
将漂洋过海去寻求和膜拜
阈限空间和杂糅身份的那位圣人
你会祝福我
你会微笑
你会告诉我

做我想做的一切
因为人生太短

2016.4

图书在版编目（CIP）数据

在郁金香的光泽中/徐怀静著. --北京: 华夏出版社，2018.9
ISBN 978-7-5080-9572-1

Ⅰ.①在… Ⅱ.①徐… Ⅲ.①诗集－中国－当代 Ⅳ.①I227

中国版本图书馆CIP数据核字（2018）第195089号

在郁金香的光泽中

作　　者	徐怀静
责任编辑	韩　平
责任印制	顾瑞清

出版发行	华夏出版社
经　　销	新华书店
印　　刷	三河市万龙印装有限公司
装　　订	三河市万龙印装有限公司
版　　次	2018年9月北京第1版 2018年9月北京第1次印刷
开　　本	880×1230　1/32
印　　张	7.5
字　　数	50千字
定　　价	58.00元

华夏出版社 网址：www.hxph.com.cn 地址：北京市东直门外香河园北里4号 邮编：100028
若发现本版图书有印装质量问题，请与我社营销中心联系调换。电话：（010）64663331（转）